Bristol Tales

Bristol Tales

ISBN 0-9549363-5-3

Published and distributed by
ENDpapers Ltd
Collage Corner, 2 Norman Court
YORK, YO1 7HU
www.endpapers.co.uk

First published November 2005
Printed by Fratelli Spada, Italy

Credits

Text

Editor:	Rachel Hazelwood
Proofreaders:	Julia Key and Ruth Wilson
Readers:	Florence Millett
	Peter Johnson

Images

ENDpapers/photography:	Graham Fellows
Cover design:	Ian Forster

Production

Design and typesetting:	gavin ward design associates
Production Manager:	Sally Mowbray
Project co-ordinator:	Florence Millett

Competition Judges

Keith Warmington	BBC Radio Bristol
Roland Clare	Bristol Grammar School
Jules Hardy	Author
Patricia Ferguson	Author
Sara Davies	Executive Producer, BBC Radio 4
Dawn Dickinson	Lecturer in Humanities, City of Bristol College
Linda Buckley	BORDERS Bookshop, Bristol

We would like to thank the staff and students of the English Department at Bristol Grammar School for their efforts and contribution to this publication.

Contents

Introduction

It's a fact: we met outside the toilets at the London Book Fair in March 2005.

One of us was sitting wearing a name badge with BRISTOL writ large, and the other one was idling, waiting for colleagues to advance in a seemingly endless queue. With books and writing uppermost in our minds – as opposed to the state of our bladders – we caught sight of one another's badges and fell to talking about the **TALES series**.

Each volume in the **TALES series** begins with one local contact, shed loads of leaflets and the launch of a writing competition. This chance encounter was the local contact and then, with Bristol, gathering in tales was easy. Why?

Firstly, Bristol is full of writers, full of creativity, full of contradiction. This creates exactly the right environment to breed short story writers.

Secondly, and for END*papers*, critically, there was a wide variety of hubs in place, with networks branching off them like spokes, that we were able to tap into.

BORDERS in Bristol, for one, is a hive of enthusiasm for creativity and a draw for local people, both to buy books and to talk about them. Many of the staff are themselves writers and they maintained a keen interest in the progress of the competition, distributing leaflets, exploiting broadcast opportunities and just generally talking up the **TALES series** whenever they could.

Bristol Grammar School is another. Unusually for volumes in the **TALES series**, we were invited to work with a school. Bristol Grammar School offered a reader service to local writers wishing to submit to the competition. This meant that a whole population of people – teachers, parents and students – could be made directly aware of **BRISTOL TALES**.

BBC Radio 4's production team for books happens to operate from Bristol. Right from the outset we had their support. Not only were senior producers able and interested to help us in promoting writing across the city, but, in addition, wherever there was a chance with local radio to promote the competition and to help make listeners aware of it, they did so.

Creative writing groups, Access and English courses in the City of Bristol College took leaflets, gave support, and generally promoted the existence of the **TALES series**. We received many submissions from them.

And then, of course, there is the great British public, which is indeterminate and unpredictable wherever competitions like this are launched. The bottom line is this: YOU NEVER KNOW.

We were lucky to find each other at the London Book Fair and the progress of the **BRISTOL TALES** has been a series of modulations on a largely successful and harmonious theme.

We are pleased with the results, delighted that Bristol has shown itself to be absolutely the hotbed of talent we expected, and we look forward to putting together another volume of **BRISTOL TALES** before too long.

Maggi Jackson
END*papers*

Lucy Shepherd
Bristol Grammar School

The Tale of the Undivided Trinity

Daniel Doherty

The time of my departure is approaching.

Nigh is the hurricane that will scatter my leaves.

Tomorrow, perhaps, the wanderer will appear,

His eye will search for me round every spot,

And will not find me.

Thomas Chatterton

1

The pale evening light casts its spell over a desolate Millennium Square as three bronze statues, one modern, two ancient, stir slowly as their shadows lengthen. Cary Grant checks his multiple reflections in the chrome-plated Imaginarium, adjusts his cummerbund, then languidly strolls over to the seated William Tyndall, still arthritically hunched over his James the First Bible.

The urbane Cary good-naturedly teases William, while William, in turn, wearily berates Cary for the shallowness and ease of his previous existence, compared to the seriousness of his own purpose in Bible translation, a passion that resulted in his being burnt at the stake. Despite their habitual banter, and their gulfs in background, they recognise that they are in this together. Cary helps William to his feet, shaking off the leaves as they proceed to an adjoining bench upon which sits Thomas Chatterton, eyes absently gazing into the middle distance, forlornly seeking inspiration from the tradesman's entrance of the Lloyds TSB Amphitheatre. He joins their conversation on the frustrations of another interminable day of inanimation.

His muse has been blighted today by a photo shoot promoting Bristol tourism. He has endured a supermodel being draped over him all day, she oblivious to his suspended animation and without a care as to the effects of her feigned intimacy upon his hormonal system. Cary bemoans the fact that whereas in Hollywood he could control his contact with fans – staging the apparent naturalness of those encounters for the lenses of sympathetic cameramen – now it seems that anyone who feels so inclined can assume familiarity, sticky fingers everywhere, posing suggestively for their clumsy amateur snaps. William laments that the visitors have no idea that his sacrifice was made to popularise the word of God. They venerate the photographic image, but are quite lost to the Word.

Our unlikely triumvirate shuffle across the square, to conduct their evening ritual. They pass through the space in the iridescent wall of mirrored water, where a mysterious process transforms their carapaces of bronze into the resplendent hues of their original clothing, their countenances assuming a pale but human pallor. Thus attired, they are prepared for their self-appointed evening task of posing as council-sponsored historical animations. They head across Anchor Square with trepidation, anxious as always lest the gigantic black beetle, ever menacing on its plinth, should learn their trick of transubstantiation.

Safely delivered to the strip of waterfront bars, Cary, ever the leader, selects for their cocktail hour the cool Californian minimalism of the Pitcher & Piano. By the door they spy a man wearing a Superman outfit. He appears quite crestfallen, as if he had fallen rather than glided from the Bristol and West building. Tables proving scarce in this popular bar, they join our fallen hero. He shifts along the table with a grunt, hoisting his belt under his ample belly, barely noticing in his self-absorption their antiquated garb, contrasting as it does with his iconic modernism. William, ever concerned, enquires as to his disposition.

Grudgingly pleased at the opportunity to share his misfortune, he explains that he is one of the founders of Fathers 4 Justice, now a nationwide movement which all began in Bristol. Today he was badly let down by so-called co-conspirators while planning to scale the Council House and hang a banner. When he tried to contact them, the new leaders from up North told him that he was now banished from their number. They gave no reason, had not even been man enough to tell him face to face, merely dumping him by text message. He growls that, though gutted, he will fight on, start up a splinter group, recover the loss of his children and his protest movement. Single-handedly if need be.

Enlivened by this show of defiance, and appreciative of their sympathetic witness, he finishes his pint, wipes his hand across his mouth, and offers them a drink. All three eagerly assent, although Tom's attention has drifted towards the group of young tourists sitting at the adjoining table. These visitors have clocked our incongruous threesome, an American among them loudly conjecturing that the guy in the bow tie may be playing Cary Grant. This flicker of attention is the signal for our costumed ones to move into their practised routine. Charismatic Cary leads, happily acknowledging the recognition. He tells them of his realisation of the American dream, from his unpromising beginnings in Bristol. He introduces William, whose life story arouses pity and respect, while a thumbnail outline of Tom's short life captures the imagination of an otherwise bored goth girl among the tourist party. She pushes Tom for details of his death, but beyond acknowledging that it may have been caused by suicide, or drug overdose, or a broken heart, he coyly refuses to elucidate the mystery further. She declares that he reminds her of the cool singer Pete Doherty, due in her view to die some day soon through excess, though commenting that despite his disreputable behaviour, he has attracted one of the world's most beautiful supermodels. Tom's imagination runs riot, thinking that if only he could break out of this daytime statue routine, then his talent for tragic romanticism could lead him into the arms of a vision of loveliness such as the model sitting on his paralysed lap today.

This girl feels emboldened to share her newfound insight that the threesome are in fact 'celebs' of yesteryear. William demurs at this sobriquet, raising a crusty eyebrow to explain that, while they may correctly be described as celebrated Bristolians, their fame is based upon substantial achievement in life, rather than the pursuit of fame as an end in itself. Cary kicks him under the table, anxious lest their source of another drink evaporates under this withering rant. In the event, they are about to lose their audience anyway, as the tourists explain with regret that they need to split if they are to catch *Beauty and the Beast* at the Hippodrome. Cary dreams wistfully of the time when he was centre stage there, performing in gripping murder mysteries, not in the phoney regurgitation of Disney cartoons. He feels immeasurably saddened that Bristolians' taste in popular culture might have come to this.

As the tourists take their final snapshot – obediently putting change into William's insistently proffered mortar board – then depart, our trinity's conversation turns to their favorite subject. Escape. As they warm to the prospect, reciting how weary they are of this routine of endlessly relating their narratives in response to the tourists' predictable questioning, our caped crusader returns at last with his tray of beers, proffering an alcopop to young Tom. They are defensive at first that should Superman – or Clark as he says he prefers to be called – know the full story, he might blow their cover and consign them permanently to brass. However, the loosening powers of the drink, and Clark's obvious relishing of conversational conspiracy in any form, encourages them to take him into their secret, and into the dilemmas they face.

His fascination grows as he hears of their painful conflict between the attractions of escape from the ignominy of permanent fossilisation in place and time, abandoned in that forsaken square, measured against the dangers attendant on their breaking out. Their principal fear and superstition of escape is that if they do not pass through the wall of mirrored water before midnight, their self-designated witching hour, then they will never again be able to enjoy all of the nightly pleasures of miraculous resurrection. A secondary but significant worry is that while they nightly grump about how comparatively easy life is for everyone in this twenty-first century – and how soft its ungrateful inhabitants have become – the reality is that they do not have the resources or the wherewithal between them to survive for the first few weeks of their release.

Clark, all his life preferring reckless action to reflective caution, impulsively offers our vacillating captives the use of his house in Montpelier while they sort themselves out. He explains that his wife left him with the house and the huge mortgage months ago to run off to Spain with the kids to join her new 'partner'. With this unimagined opportunity of shelter and support, a new mood is suddenly upon them. In a heartbeat, our trio break out of their habitual defeatist conversation and begin to talk excitedly about new possibilities. Mobilising themselves before they can change their minds, they pick up Will's takings and scurry out behind Clark, fleeing over the Piro Bridge towards Christmas Steps, up and over towards their fate in Montpelier.

Clark's surprisingly capacious terraced house is all they could have asked for, situated in an anonymous street up a hill where no one would think to find them. The hour before midnight passes painfully slowly. Clark whiles away the time by telling tales, showing photos of his deeds of derring-do during his Fathers 4 Justice days. They are impressed by a press cutting of his defiant stand atop the Clifton Suspension Bridge, feeling inwardly somewhat ashamed of their own cowardly fears of mortality. After all, they had each faced painful death before, and knew through this strange reincarnation that there was the possibility of life beyond. As the mantelpiece clock strikes twelve, they regard each other in wonder, realising that they are still here, on this twenty-first century earth, vibrantly and palpably alive. Clark beams as they ecstatically clap his back, delighted that he has eventually effected liberation for someone after the entire frustrating impasse of Fathers 4 Justice. As the excitement subsides, he adopts a practical stance, proposing that tomorrow he will make a plan to ensure that they become happily assimilated townspeople, their statuesque identities eradicated.

The next morning, Cary throws open his curtains, seeing a

building that looks somehow familiar. Of course, it is his old school, Fairfield, a place of painful memory. He can only hope that the new building he sees by the highway might be a replacement for this monument to childhood oppression. The smell of bacon lures him downstairs, where Clark is showcasing the clothes he bought during his early morning foray to the St Peter's Hospice shop on Cotham Hill. They giggle as they try on this miscellaneous garb. Clark then lines them up for the mandatory hair dye procedure in the shower. Tom chooses black with a crimson streak, offset by a hoody top to complete his fashionable disguise. William looks forward to his new pair of spectacles.

Over breakfast, they discuss their plans for the day. Tom is directed towards Cotham Porter Stores cider house, where Clark has a Fathers 4 Justice contact who will provide them with fresh identities. Mulling over new names, Tom goes for Tom Rowley, after the medieval poet he so imaginatively created long ago; Will chooses the name Martin Luther, a modernising reformer whom he met and much admired; Grant plumps for Cary Leach, to his ear a pleasing amalgam of his old and new identities.

They alight the pavement with a happy tread, delighting in the freshness of their first morning of freedom. Armed with a Bristol map, they roll down the hill, seeking their way across Stokes Croft towards the Porter Stores. Walking the streets, they are astonished by the diversity of people they encounter. Tentatively enquiring in the pub where they might find their contact, named simply Len, Tom is directed towards a table down the far end of the bar. He explains his purpose to Len, to be told that business can indeed be done, but only if he removes his hood. Cary and William snigger a little at this, leaving him to his nefarious transactions while they head for Whiteladies Road, a thoroughfare holding fond memories for them both.

William points to the rash of charity shops at the bottom of Cotham Hill, surprised yet pleased that modern commerce seems geared mainly around giving. Cary enviously eyes a dinner suit in the window of one, anticipating the joys of sartorial freedom. Meandering past the BBC building, Cary reads a sign inviting citizens to audition for a reality show called 'Escape Bristol'. He gently explains to William that the temptation is irresistible, he simply must go inside. William is in fact pleased to have some time alone, to meditate on what purpose he might bring to his new life. He pauses outside the University Tower on Queen's Road, standing out among the throng of smoking students, while he reflects on whether the academic pursuit of ancient languages and history might make a welcome respite from Christian fellowship. And yet, despite all the pain that was inflicted upon him by fellow Christians, the tug of the Church remains compelling. With a sigh for the scholarly fascinations that might have been, he shuffles down Park Street, squinting at its incongruous mix of indie music, high fashion and strait-laced religious stores, past the windowless Masonic Hall, towards the cathedral, which is set back off the refreshing greensward of College Green.

A board outside proclaims 'The Cathedral Church of the Holy and Undivided Trinity'. He is dismayed at this continuing promulgation of impenetrable liturgical nonsense when what the Church has always needed is to reach out, as he once put it, to 'every ploughman in the land'. Hesitating before entering, fearful lest he discover more of this alienating, superior language within, a young black woman with a beatific smile approaches. Confidently, eagerly, she invites him to join in the Elim Church celebrations, whose joyous mission is to 'make the Bible relevant'. She quotes Mandela's inaugural speech from the Church's colourful values statement: "Who am I to be brilliant, gorgeous, talented and fabulous? Actually, who are you not to be? You are a child of God."

She directs him towards a marquee on the green that spontaneously erupts to the sound of glorious gospel song, filling the air with foot-tapping invitation. William knows he has met his Damascene moment. He struggles with his resistance, then surrenders to her beckoning, as they walk side by side towards the marquee.

Two months later, all three keep their Sunday lunchtime appointment at the Coronation Tap in Clifton to celebrate their benefactor, Clark's, birthday. Keith Warmington of Radio Bristol is playing some redemptive live blues, amid a warm and friendly atmosphere. Over a glass of Exhibition Cider, cautiously supped, they share their recent adventures. Cary preens himself, telling of how he sailed through his audition, despite the yellow hair and fake glasses, and will be on a TV near you soon, his ultimate ambition to become a film critic. He has made the Pineapple pub his local, he says, because of the quality of the pasties there. Tom is eager to relay how his trip to the Porter Stores yielded not only passports, but also a lead to Christchurch Studios, situated next door to the Tap, where Massive Attack record. Len introduced him to a goth band, formerly known as 'Lupine Howl', which is now enjoying reformation – as all good bands and faiths do – under the name 'Marvelous Boy', with Tom as lyricist. And no, he hadn't met any supermodels yet, but he is dating a comely hairdresser from Guy Henri whom he is sure will become one.

William rhapsodises on his discovery of evangelism, his happy smile reflecting an inner radiance that takes years off his previously burdened features. Clark, happily acknowledging their birthday felicitations, sheepishly confides that when passing through Stokes Croft, he bumped into William outside his Elim chapel. Reluctant at first to accept the inward invitation, he is now a regular visitor, considering – to his own amazement – involvement in the children's Sunday School. He had talked to both his children that morning, hearing them giggle their way through 'Happy Birthday', and his heart is glad. He muses that he feels a different person from the embittered protestor of two months ago.

Keith plays a poignant song with the chorus 'I feel like a worn-out engine, I have lost my driving wheel'. Cary sings along, then declares that far from losing their driving wheels, he feels that this merry band have found theirs anew, after a long, directionless period in the wilderness. They look back on their previous existence, fondly remembering those antiquated celebrities arrested in time, a bizarre juxtaposition of characters separated by centuries while tantalisingly trapped in a new one, yet quite unable to fully engage with all it had to offer. Clark pulls out a copy of the *Evening Post*, pointing to the headline: 'MILLENNIUM STATUE THEFT RIDDLE REMAINS UNSOLVED. NEW CASTINGS COMMISSIONED BY COUNCIL.'

The byline tells of the police abandoning hope of finding them, believing that a private collector commissioned this audacious theft. The outcry over their disappearance means that the statues will be replaced, only this time with increased security, including the placement of cameras. Cary chortles that his second reincarnation would not know whether to laugh or cry at being permanently on camera, or know what to think when the bronze was poured once more into the central casting. None of them could predict whether the fountain's magic would continue to work, or if their successors would come alive every evening, as had happened to them so miraculously since their first day of installation. William sits bolt upright, dumbstruck by a flashback from those earliest times. Finding the words to speak, he whispers that at that moment of installation, he heard the sound of gospel singing from the nearby Anchor Square. It floated through the gap in the fountain, as it eased their transit into this new era.

Hens' Tales

Lyssa Randolph

For all that it's dark

The city's routine claustrophobia lifts

As you tack across Queen Square

To where the harbour's laced

With isobars of neon,

Cash burning a hole in your pocket,

Desire like one in your guts.

'Nighttown' Tom Phillips (Bristol 2004)

It is a Saturday evening at the end of June and the last one before I'll be married. I'm standing on the cobbles outside a new restaurant-bar on Welsh Back where I've been told to come. It's decorated with brightly coloured waves, turquoise and cornflower blue, to give it a Mediterranean look because it's overlooking the water. From its sets of aluminium tables and chairs under big blue parasols, you can see the cabin cruisers and tourist boats that seem to belong to another, watery city of which I have no part. Cars rumble past on the cobbles. Over on the bridge, buses ferry in those who claim the town centre for the night. I feel a tug of anticipation, a skip of the heart. This is my city: small, knowable, intimate. With each return its facets change as those on a paper consequences teller change with the quick fingers of a child. Each time I've returned it has offered up some new facet with a different story. Each has its place for me. If I shiver it is because of the breeze tracing through the plane trees.

I see you as we approach the mooring place. You appear assured and relaxed, Annie, like a tourist in your white sundress, sat on a silver chair like the ones in Plaza Real, as you survey the scene around Bristol Bridge. Your back towards me, your gaze out on the dock. The group is in high spirits, ready to surprise you. Your sister says to me, we'll hold her, Nadia, while you knot the rope around her middle, and she laughs, and we begin your abduction onto the boat that is already laden and waiting.

My sister leads a crowd of my friends running towards me and I start up, my chair falling behind me. I hadn't imagined this: the warm ache high in my chest as the deep pleasures of familiarity envelop me, drawing close together a group already crowded with memories. Their laughing faces are made strange with their masquerade: they are all pirates. Most of my old friends are here: I recognise Nadia from her laughter; she is decked out in velvet breeches and high, laced boots, a stiff white cotton embroidered shirt buttoned up high, her chest heavy with bead necklaces and silver, with a gold plastic sword wedged through a wide belt. Her deception is complete with her long brown beard and a leather three-cornered hat; behind her beard she is laughing. But after that night, I realise she wasn't as she seemed.

Nadia and Lily cry out that they are to take me to the waiting boat below. I, lashed with rope, am a maiden for the pirate marauders. The ritual is played out with mock violence and comic determination. I'm laughing and crying, tears are running into my hair. I step down into this narrow boat that is meant for me all along. Lily reaches out and smoothes my hair away from my face and a bundle is passed to her, a mesh of white net sprinkled with the glitter of sequins. She arranges the shape on my head, somehow attached to a hair band, patting it into the semblance of a bride's veil. I feel strangely exposed in my white cotton dress and unlike myself, like a photograph of myself as a child at a birthday party. An instinctual cry goes up from the girls, syncopated, a triumphant tribal chorus, and immediately three corks whoosh from the wine bottles like fireworks. I'm being carried away, out of the city and out of my self.

Lily and I have herded our band of twelve onto the boat: come together to celebrate and mark your voyage into a new world. You are the first of our circle to be married, yet it is not an unbroken circle. With this journey we're all to forgive foolish acts and the rivalries of the past. I, too, wish this evening could bind us. Here, I could be suspended from the everyday.

Summer after summer that I've spent in the shabby heat of the city, and I didn't know about this: never felt the easy movement of a boat pushing out up the river past homes, warehouses, masses of green overhanging willows and impatient moorhens steering into secret banks.

You once said that you are happiest when you are able to put down roots; that your favourite journey is always the one home; that you only know who you are when you are surrounded by the known. Adrift from the city, now you are in limbo between identities. You're setting yourself apart from the group, but you're not yet a wife.

I'm surprised at all the photos of me, copied large and flagged out inside the boat like a series of maps for me to chart. Me and Lily in Grandma's garden, matching in our Clothkits outfits. Me with Nadia wearing roller boots and ra-ra skirts outside her house, probably the age when we first met. These brightly coloured, spotlit moments in my life are isolated from others and escape true memory and its slippery pale scenes. There, a much later picture of us and some of the others, all dressed in white, short dresses or halter-neck tops and trousers, Nadia wearing her favourite turquoise necklace, and laughing in a restaurant somewhere on a Greek island. The photo has become the substance of the memory itself, with far more detail than a true memory could furnish; the events of that time, of that holiday, evade me. I try to concentrate, will the memory into life, but there is no visceral response, no chain firing in the brain. Guilt creeps in, an unwelcome guest. I know I should remember what the event was, or even where exactly it was. I wouldn't dare ask Nadia to talk about the holiday – she might remind me of something I'd rather forget.

I remember the surprise that my face must have betrayed when you told me that you were getting married. But with your evident happiness the sting faded. I too got swept up in your enthusiasm. Your wedding took on its own gentle momentum and inexorable direction, like the boat. I'd never thought about marriage, even when we were younger, it wasn't ever in our thoughts. Well, it wasn't in mine. For me it was always what other people did, perhaps when they were older, but always older than we were, Annie. But now, of course, we have reached the proper age, as if having taken the wrong path and arrived here somewhat by accident.

The sun lights up the figures against the water, linked on the deck in knots, glasses of cava in hand. You are nodding in answer to someone's question, your eyes slightly closed, receptive and enjoying the attention, the girls stroking your arms and kissing your face, rapt as a cat in the bright evening sunlight. It illuminates your hair, burnishing your veil like a huge and voluptuous strange flower. They stumble and cluster around you, mewing like kittens and pressing close for warmth, to enjoy your talismanic protection, the solidity you represent.

Old friendships may be relished and renewed, acquaintances can be warmed rapidly to intimacy in the hothouse of this boat. Our own strong bonds are stretched taut to accommodate my recent return. Neither you nor home can stay the same. How subtly and deeply this change has come; a change both as rapid and yet as gradual as the painful tearing of ligament and skin in the gravid bow of a mother's belly. But always with change comes loss. At the feast of your new identity, loss is attendant like an abject and hungry stray dog. I feel it bite and gnaw.

I'm slightly uneasy in this beam of intensity, the scrutiny of the crowd of girls pinning me in its white glare, each of them dosing me with rum and singing "What's it like, what's it like to give all your love to just one man?" Lily has insisted upon our recitation of my past loves, and although I resent it to begin with, I submit. The rum burns my throat and begins to lighten my limbs, warming my heart and easing the talk. We laugh together at some of the more unlikely boys, and at my efforts to recall all their names, as I slowly thread them out like coloured beads onto a string before them. Nadia's face is blank as she moves closer to me and tucks my hair back gently, arranging the veil behind me. Her unsmiling face belies her tender gesture, but I can still read it. It is a numbness that I've seen before, but not for me. Her boyfriends, like my own, came and went, not usually staying long. Rather than nursing the hurt aloud and prodding at the tenderness, she would become remote, impassive. Her fingers stray into my hair, stroking mechanically. What was once so easy, a close fit, an instinct for intimacy between us despite the distances, has become worn and frayed. But she could change that.

"Here's a bottle of the finest rum, milady," they chorus, now in growly, salty sea dog voices, and the real drinking begins as the first glass is placed in your hands. Conversations are abandoned while they fete you with a chorus of "ho ho ho and a bottle of rum", but no one really knows the words. Some are pinning large paper phalluses to your veil, while you smile serenely and shrug; others nod vigorously and are laughing drunkenly. You draw presents from your lucky dip box; no prophylactics here, you say, waving a beribboned packet of Pregnacare. You are freer than ever. The closer the dense knot of girls presses down, the lighter you become. You are in, but no longer of, the circle: this is the protection and freedom your identity offers you. I catch hold of the edge of your veil in an effort to anchor you, fingers caught in your hair, to stop you floating away altogether.

Intermittent peeps of moorhen and coot reach us in the twilight; they are startled by our boat's turning, and I feel momentarily sad as if a spell is fading and I must ready myself for a return to an ordinary shape, no longer this princess bride. We pass another boat, larger than ours, that seems to come too close. The passengers have an uncanny white glow in the gloom that matches the ghostliness of my own costume. On deck are a group of masked men. They're stormtroopers. In their midst, Darth Vader stands, taller than the others and dressed in the black uniform and black mask. There are lewd exchanges, and piratical bravado, waving of swords and bottles of wine. "The force is strong in these ones," pronounces one of the men loudly and soberly; another cries, "Do you want to see my Bristol Packet?" Lily leans right over the edge of the boat and offers to let them stroke her beard; others blow coy kisses while assuming obscene poses. Darth Vader asks for me, but they refuse to give me up: "you are our prize, our maiden," they chant.

You are standing, statuesque at the bow, watching behind us, like a figurehead in reverse, your veil standing out stiffly. At last we're turning back into the harbour in the darkness. We pass the roofless church floodlit on Castle Green, glide underneath one of the arches of Bristol Bridge, girls' voices echoing. As we pass other pleasure boats, we drift in and out of contact with them, enclosed in our own close world where confidences have been exchanged and hard and high laughter builds. Turning away from the knot of girls, I pass to the side of the boat, press against the edge and look out at the glittering promises of the waterside bars cast up brokenly on the dark water. The city has never looked so beautiful to me; neon pink and blue, silver and green phosphorescence dance in the blackness.

Time rushes up to meet us. We're already docking at Welsh Back: my sister commandeers the party, barking that all must walk the plank, my hearties, though her voice is rather hoarse now, and lacking in authority. I'm on solid ground and rather relieved. I love everyone, I'm filled with love for the smallest gestures that their hands and voices convey. I wish all could be made anew with this journey, lives braided and rebraided. And Nadia as before. Not blank, and blind to her defensiveness.

I know that my voice has gone too high, but I can't stop laughing. I can hear the laughter coming from me, almost disembodied; I feel light, very light. The others are bunching up and suddenly I'm taken up in the surge down Crow Lane, where we catch sight of a mirrored wall that makes grotesques of us: pretty men and bearded ladies. Lily brandishes a bunch of bananas she has brought, and they are passed around. The girls line up, position me in the centre, and assume poses ready for the camera.

They make a show in front of the mirror panels. Someone passes around your pink lipstick, Annie; they are painting pouting lips below pencilled black eyeliner moustaches. The dissembling feeds their desire. They are saying, "Perhaps we might meet the stormtroopers again." At that moment you turn to me, take my hand and grip it tightly. You sway slightly as if still aboard the boat, and pull me into the frame. Lily takes a group photograph, crushed together in drunken embraces. Thus you inscribe each other with your pleasurable illusions. You always said that photographs restricted your ability to see the past clearly. You'll choose to remember this moment without the blurred image, Annie, yet without knowing your own memory to be a testament to delusion. You let go of my hand and are whirled away along Queen Charlotte Street, dancing between two pirates. The sense of loss rushes in through a slamming door and bites.

The only girlish one among the bearded ladies, I lead the band; the narrow streets are wide open to us. I'm strolling, not stopping at the new, tawdry bars wedged between the faded pomposity of 1970s offices and smart Georgian brick facades. High buildings totter and give way to night sky as we come out on Queen Square, its looming plane trees shivering in the light, warm wind. The square is almost deserted, a large, neat green quadrangle scored with white gravel paths which crunch underfoot as the pirates tear up its dignified repose. In the rush to the centre of the square they gallop in a mime of horse riding and doff their hats to the statue on horseback. Someone before us has placed a traffic cone on the statue's head. We tack across to the teeming city centre.

Recognising our own tribe, we see other hen parties scattered across the city centre, wending their way between the sunken fountains which overflow with bubble bath from some joker's handbag. The ribbed wooden boards with footlights, built over the hidden river's power, run slanting towards the harbour edge. At this moment it seems a stage of sound and light for the shows of ribald courtship and clamorous friendship played out nightly. A ward of nurses, the hemline of their dresses re-stitched higher to show stocking tops, outfits miniaturised like dolls. A drift of angels, their pink nylon wired wings erect and jaunty, sing in perfect soprano and alto harmony, the bride's descant trilling over the top like birdsong. We wave and laugh, communicating a common purpose and pleasure, before they move away under the structure of fake wooden masts and canvas and flutter into Corn Street. Perhaps their presence feeds our dream that we all belong to this night and to each other.

I look for Nadia but she's vanished. At least, she seems not to be with us any more. Had she even left the party when we docked? Did she leave at Queen Square? A jolt of anxiety twists me. No one else seems to notice her absence. For a moment I turn to Lily to ask has she seen her, but a sort of hot, palpable relief spreads through me and just as quickly I turn away again. A small voice in my head urges my right to the pleasures of the moment. I try to lose myself in the group. Arms slip through mine and buoy me up from my regrets. Then we feel the ardour of the swelling crowd, press it close to our hearts, and sail on up Park Street and into our own bit of collective history.

Charlie's Tale

Alan Toyne

Women and cats, if you compulsion use,

The pleasure which they die for will refuse.

Thomas Chatterton

"How are you, love? How's your new little basement flat?" My mother's voice echoes down the receiver. "What on earth is that frightful noise?"

I look at myself in the reflection of the kitchen windows, sitting with my feet up on one of my new rattan chairs, surrounded by boxes and discarded newspaper. I'm wearing a baggy old T-shirt and a pair of leggings, my hair is pulled back in a ponytail and I have big bags under my eyes. Mum would have a fit if she could see me now.

"I'm fine Mum, just unpacking the kitchen things."

"You should make yourself a nice cup of tea, Sarah. That's the first thing to do when you move in somewhere new."

I salute my reflection with a large glass of red wine.

"Is that the washing machine you've got going?" she continues. "It sounds like you're living in a train station."

"No, it's the old lady upstairs." A fly, having sought refuge in my flat to escape the sun, now bats against the light bulb beneath the throbbing ceiling.

"At this time of night? I hope she's not going to be a neighbour from hell. We might see you on the telly."

"The landlord says she spends all day sitting at the window waiting for her husband."

"Does he work nights?"

"No. Apparently he ran off years ago with somebody else."

"Oh, how tragic. Try not to think about it. You're always welcome back here love, isn't she John? You know that, don't you?" I picture Dad sitting in his armchair peering at the Sunday paper through his dusty glasses.

Her voice drops to whisper, "I think she's feeling a bit lonely down there in Bristol. You know, missing Jason."

"You're welcome back here, Sarah," my dad yells, through miles of telephone cable from Buckingham.

"She's about to make herself a nice cup of tea."

"I'll speak to you tomorrow, let you know how my first day at work goes."

"All right darling, if you're sure you're all right."

I empty the bottle of wine into my glass and salute my reflection again. Jason took the matching glass as we divided up our possessions back in Wandsworth.

A cat alights on the window ledge outside and I slurp wine down my chin. It rubs its tabby coat against the glass and opens its mouth in a silent mew.

I get up and walk into the tiny lounge. Where to start? The floor is covered with boxes sealed with brown parcel tape. Dad has written 'Books' on them and 'CDs'. I have a lampshade somewhere that we bought in Thailand. It would be perfect in the kitchen. The cat flap rattles and I see the tabby mog peering around the cream painted doorframe.

"Come in. Make yourself at home, why don't you?"

The cat sits down and splays its back legs, to lick its chest.

"I'm going to have to sleep on the couch tonight. Can't see us reassembling a futon, can you?"

The cat continues to lick.

Jason and I had spent a weekend when we got back from Thailand, making our bedroom reminiscent of our holiday. We had bought a dark wooden table in Bangkok and some triangular red and blue cushions, embroidered with gold thread. Jason had a photograph of the sunrise on Ko Samui enlarged and we hung it on the wall. The headboard, bowed in defeat at our sexless partnership, was chucked out, along with the springy mattress. A load of kids jumped on it in the street amongst the piled smelly rubbish bags, warmed by the sun. We got a futon back from Ikea all the way from Wilsden or somewhere on the Tube.

"How come I got this knackered futon and he walked off with the table?"

The cat has disappeared. I look through the kitchen door

and see it sitting on the table. The tumble dryer still rumbles through the ceiling and the cat's head twitches as its eyes follow the tired fly, bouncing around the light bulb.

"I'm going to bed." I see my mobile next to a pile of cookery books. "Better set the alarm. You'll get dizzy doing that, you stupid cat."

I go into my new bathroom and reach for the light cord. I brush the cold shower curtain instead. The light is by a tiny cupboard above the sink. It hums into life as I click on my toothbrush. The bristles whizz against my teeth and I find a tube of toothpaste with no lid in the cupboard. I switch off my toothbrush, and hear a frantic buzzing in the kitchen. The cat is sitting on the table with a weird smile on its face. Its eyes are half closed and its tail flicks. The buzzing comes from its mouth. I look up at the light bulb, but the fly has gone. The cat opens its eyes as the fly crunches between its teeth.

"Goodnight, you freak. You're just what I need, a sadistic insect-torturing flatmate. Let yourself out."

I flop onto the couch. The duvet smells damp as I shut out the street lamp glare.

Fremantle Square. A family sat on the grass all day as I unpacked the car, cooking sausages and listening to a tinny radio. The children were told to, "Stop pissing on that nice red phonebox and go behind the bloody tree."

The Georgian houses painted in pastel colours peered down at them through sash windows.

A shadow crosses my curtains in the garden outside. My new possessions appear out of the semi-darkness, the flat-packed Ikea wardrobe and yet-to-be-assembled shelves.

"Charlie. Where are you?" a shrill voice calls. "Come on Charlie, come home. Your dinner's ready."

I dislodge the warm cat from the couch.

"I hope you haven't got fleas." I step across the scratchy carpet and pull back the curtains. A woman, her plastic raincoat shining orange in the lamplight, stands at the top of my steps, her nose pointing at the stars.

I fumble with the front door. "Hello. Are you all right?"

Her head swivels towards me.

"It's Elsie isn't it?" She has long, striped men's pyjamas on. "I'm Sarah. I've just moved in."

The old lady peers down at me through large round glasses.

"My Charlie's gone and left me." She glances out across the square. The houses are quiet, their windows hooded with heavy curtains.

"Would you like a cup of tea?" Why the hell did I offer that?

"Could I come in and use your phone?" She clasps the railing running down my steps. Her veins flex beneath translucent skin. "I should tell someone he's gone. The police, maybe the fire brigade?"

"You'll have to excuse the mess. I'm halfway through unpacking."

Elsie wheezes her way through my lounge and I follow her into the kitchen.

"Are you married?" She flops into a chair at the table.

"No."

She frowns. "Not like the girls that lived here before, I hope?"

"I've just come out of a four year relationship in London." I pour water into the kettle.

She deflates, the coat hanging off her bony frame. "That's males for you." She catches her reflection in the window. "They always up and leave in the end. Demand things from you for years."

Her eyebrows are drawn onto her head way too high.

"Red-blooded," he used to say. "I'm a red-blooded male. I can't help it."

I rummage in a box for some mugs. "Um, how do you take your tea?"

"Black. Charlie likes milk. Can't abide my black tea. So he ups and leaves me."

Back in Wandsworth the cooker used to wink out the time in green digital figures. The dials on my chipped electric hob look back at me blankly.

"Do you think he'll come back?" I put her cup on the table. I hope she likes it hot.

"Oh, he'll be back. He always comes back, then runs off again. Red-blooded males. All trooping in and out of here. They used to come through the back gate late at night and leave through your front door." She looks into my empty wine glass at the trail of sediment. "You got a job?"

"I'm a nurse." I lower a cardboard box entitled 'Knives, Forks and Spoons etc' to the floor and sit down opposite her. "I'm starting at the BRI tomorrow morning."

Her hand jerks, the tea stops midway to her puckered mouth. "Well." She glares. "I shan't keep you then."

"Oh. But your tea. Are you sure you're okay?"

"Yes, I'm quite all right, thank you." She wobbles to her feet and I follow her to the front door.

"Well goodnight then." I hold the door for her. "I'd go straight to bed if I were you."

"Red-blooded males," she mutters as she pulls her way up my steps. At the top she looks down through her glasses at me. "My sister claimed to be a nurse," she hisses.

"Right. Goodnight." I shut her out and hear the rattle of her front door above.

"Charlie. Come in, love."

The couch is still warm, as if Jason had just got up to go to work after one of my night shifts. I snuggle under the duvet and the cat flap rattles again. The cat lands on the arm of the couch and begins to purr. Upstairs the tumble dryer rumbles into life.

The sun is out when I leave work. I walk across the car park at the back of the hospital. My new *Bristol A-Z* is in my bag but I don't want to use it. I cross over a steep hill and walk down a narrow street shaded with limp sycamore branches. The city stretches out below, a bowl of streets and houses. Cars churn up the M32 to the M4 and London. Jason would go mad when I got the *Lonely Planet* out in Thailand. He said it made us look like tourists. We'd spend hours wandering deserted back streets at night looking for a hotel he'd memorised on a map in his head.

"Hiya. It's Sarah, isn't it?"

I shade my eyes.

A curly-haired guy looks down at me. "We met today in Radiology. I'm Simon."

"Yeah, hi. I was miles away. Do you live around here?"

"No, I wish." He falls into pace with me. "I'm down in Bedminster sharing a house with a load of other nurses. I'm off to meet a friend of mine in the pub."

A flight of steps leads down to a square, where a group of drunks sit on a bench with white legs poking out of rolled up trousers.

"You live in this neck of the woods then?" His Adam's apple rolls up his throat as he talks.

"Yeah, Fremantle Square. It's just up here somewhere. I moved in yesterday."

"No way! Phil lives in Fremantle Square. I'm meeting him in the Hare on Hill. Must be your local."

We start up the steps, sloped between tall houses, flowers drooping over the garden walls, and turn into a cobbled street. A terraced garden with an iron gate across it is overrun with orange petals and tiny blue flowers, hanging from faded pots. The house opposite has shiny floorboards and a stuffed bookcase, framed by tall windows. The front door is green with a brass letterbox.

"I think we've come up a road too high, the pub's down there somewhere." Simon bounces his hand across the black spear-tip fencing. "Do you fancy a drink?"

"Yeah. Great." I feel out of breath; London is so flat, not a hill in sight. "Is Phil a nurse too?"

"No. I always try to mix with a non-hospital person once a week. Present company excepted of course. It keeps you sane."

The pavement drops to the cobbles in long steps. "This is the back of Fremantle Square," I say. "I think that's my flat."

"With that weird purple tree in the garden?" Simon grins. "The pub's just down here then, I think."

"Cheers." I clink my glass against their pints.

"And only a minute from my front door," Phil says. "Yours too, I suppose. What number are you?"

"Number four. I'm in the basement flat." Phil has a ponytail and wears a denim jacket.

"You're underneath that batty bloody woman. Did you hear her yelling last night?" He taps a Marlboro Light onto the table. It has a white filter.

"You mean Elsie. I invited her in for a cup of tea."

"You should have dosed it with arsenic."

"That's a bit harsh isn't it mate?" Simon has froth on his lip.

"That's easy for you to say." Phil lights his cigarette and shoots smoke from his nostrils; it uncurls in the sunlight. "You two with your weird nursing hours. Some of us need to get a good night's kip without being woken to the squeaky cries of 'Charlie. Come home'."

"Charlie's her husband," I say. "He ran off and left her for another woman."

"I was told he ran off with her sister." Phil taps ash onto the floor. He is drinking Waggledance. Why would anyone drink a beer called Waggledance? "I always thought she was looking for her cat. She asked me for change for the phone the other day too. The night we get a good night's sleep in this place will be about a week before you smell something horrible coming from upstairs."

"Come on, mate. You don't want to put Sarah off." Simon grins. "She's only just moved in."

"I heard your flat used to be a brothel too, but that's another story."

"Another red wine?" Simon interjects.

"I'll have another one." Phil gulps down the last third of his pint. "I do feel sorry for the old bag. Poor thing spends all day looking out the window. Only leaves the house to spook out the locals. You should see her in the moonlight in her bloody raincoat, she looks like the scuttling dwarf in that fucking freaky movie. You know the one in Venice?"

"Don't Look Now, isn't it?"

"Yeah. You should see her, sometimes she wears three hats at once, one on top of the other." He lights another cigarette; they are duty-free ones from Belgium.

"She had her washing machine going all last night, after she left my flat."

"You see Si. Sarah's had enough of her already and she only moved in last night."

"You guys could always move to Bedminster, share a house with a pack of nurses, our street's full of them. You'd save a fortune too, you must pay a bomb living up here."

"The landlord can't charge you much," Phil smiles, "living beneath her. I reckon she keeps all the smackheads down in Stokes Croft away, haunting the place in her nightwear, or could be they're just too fucked to walk up the hill. I'm going for a piss. You getting those drinks in mate or what?"

Simon rolls his eyes. "He goes off on one sometimes, reckons he's hilarious."

"She thinks her husband keeps coming back and then deserting her again." I finish my wine.

"Christ. Ending up alone at the end of it all with Alzheimer's." Simon stands up and fishes his wallet out of his jeans. "Him going off with her sister, doesn't bear thinking about. Still, it could be worse."

I raise an eyebrow.

"She could live in my street."

I sit cross-legged in front of my shelves. I like to group my books in a seamless train of thought, *The Star of the Sea* next to Tony Hawks and his travels *Round Ireland with a Fridge*. I pick the *Lonely Planet Thailand* guide out of the box. I'd looked at the *Lonely Planet England* guide last week. It had said 'Bristol is buzzing'.

"Charlie. Charlie, I know you're in there." Elsie bangs on my front door, her voice muffled by my washing machine spinning in the kitchen.

"Buzzing with flies and demented old women." My legs ache as I stand to open the door. "What's the matter, Elsie?"

"You've got my Charlie in there with you." She pushes past me with fragile arms. "You nurses are all the same. Small wonder you moved in here, all those floozies before you." Her eyes are big and watery behind her glasses.

"Elsie, no one's here. I've just moved in, remember?"

She sails across to the kitchen door. "I knew it."

The cat is sitting on top of my washing machine, a nasty relic from the seventies that matches my cooker. It shakes and judders on the floor. The cat smiles, its eyes half closed. It must have another fly in its mouth buzzing against its yellow teeth. I glance down. The cat's penis, erect and shiny, pokes from its furry hood.

"Wretched red-blooded males. Always leaving you to get it

elsewhere." The cat's eyes widen as Elsie grabs it round the middle. "Come home to me, Charlie. I know how to take care of you best."

"I'm sorry. I thought he was a stray."

"Hear that, Charlie?" She strokes the cat's ears. "She's leading you astray."

"What? I won't let him in again. He just came in last night through the cat flap and got on the couch with me."

She wobbles out of the flat leaving me in the kitchen. The washing machine comes to a halt and I hear the phone ringing.

"Hello dear, how are you?"

"Hi Mum."

"Your father and I were thinking. Why don't you get a cat? Didn't you say your flat has a cat flap?"

I push a box of saucepans across the back door and sit on it.

A Tale of Angel Wings and Wine

Philip Jarvis

*This story was inspired by a quote from a
local graffiti artist. Looking at the art and
realising it's graffiti, you question why you
should think it's important, then you realise
it's not a question of what's there,
it's what you've perceived that really matters.
Sometimes you remember to forget things when
all you need to do is hold on to those moments.*

Philip Jarvis

The walk home was usually more uplifting than it was that night. The rain fell with a ferocity that was often only seen mirrored in the people in the city centre on a drunken, brawly Saturday night. It cascaded down through Bishopston, washing away the detritus of the streets, intertwining streams of spring dancing teasingly around each other, joining each other, becoming more whole. Underneath a tree, trying to keep out of the rain, was an angel. She stopped me and asked directions for a part of town that was on my route, so I said I'd show her the way and we started walking together. I didn't feel that this was the time for questions of faith or belief, so instinctively I ignored them and lit up a cigarette. She asked if she could have one. I obliged. What else can you do when an angel asks for a Lucky Strike?

She stopped in one of the numerous Gloucester Road off-licences on the way. Emerging with more bottles of red wine than such a fragile creature could possibly carry, let alone drink, we set off again. I procured an equal share of the weight while she ripped into the screw-top bottle and started to quaff straight from the bottle. Not angelic behaviour at all. Why was an angel walking around the Gloucester Road, chugging red wine from the bottle, on the way to a dive, walking with me?

"I got drunk on the job," she answers without me having to ask her anything. This deviant inebriate, the redundant drunkard, was as far removed from any host of heaven that I could have imagined. She started crying, almost wincing with every word that I thought and every gesture that I made.

"What use am I? I whisper, I yell, I paw, I can't do this any more." She rhymed as basically as a psalm. Idiosyncrasies of speech from a previous era fell over each plosive and lyrical syllable. Listening to her was like listening to a rose reciting Rollins. "I'm going to get drugs to help get me away from myself. These wings are dead weight when you no longer believe in grace. The little happiness I spread is so thin it may as well be dead. It only occurs during my forgotten moments when I neglect to remember that anyone's watching."

We walked in silence a bit further, her wings getting tragically caught in the brambles above her. She flustered a little, composed herself and broke down, cradling her head in her hands, sobbing uncontrollably. No one could see this wasted, sacred angel crying, the tears mixed into the rain streaming down her face, the intertwining rivers of pain and nature embracing each other. We sat down in Montpelier train station, the sounds of the city barely audible through the slow whisper of the train tracks and the harsh cleansing of the rain.

"When was the last time you loved?" she asked me. I never expected a tatty wino to be so coherent and direct, but I suppose you must make exceptions for angels hanging around Montpelier. She sat next to me on the cold, metallic bench. Her back curved into a slouch, sandaled feet curling into themselves, white dress not so much flowing as flailing. The dress had evidently seen better days. The hem at the bottom had worn away and straggles of heavenly cotton were dreadlocked in the dirty water. Her arms looked emaciated, pinprick scars jutting out at marginal distances. I got the feeling that they weren't there for the drugs she craved, more out of a ritual. Her feathers were matted and her halo crooked. Her hair was also dreadlocked in the rain. It kept flopping in front of her face, covering her matte bright blue eyes and she kept shoving it behind her ears, sniffling, crying outright at her own impotence and her inability to keep control of her hair, let alone anything else.

Instead of answering, I thought I'd show her. I held her hand and motioned her up. Her body was heavy, unwilling to move into tomorrow.

"We can run away," I said, answering her question in an oblique way. People are always desperate at train stations, desperate to leave, to return, to see loved ones; desperate in so many different ways. Here was not the place for a desperate angel desperate for a fleeting solution. She looked up at me, her eyes dulled. She looked at me through eyes of the past, not seeing the future.

"You tell me things I understand," she said, almost reading my thoughts. "I mean, there aren't simpler ideas than that. Sometimes our language fails us when we're trying to tell an idea. Maybe it's just a lack of articulation, maybe it is the language, but it always ends up being so hard trying to talk to people about something they might not understand," she concluded, sounding more secure in her lack of any truths. Her slurring had reached a point where it was difficult to decide if she was being serious about the impossibility of serious connection through communication.

It was a vain situation. In that moment there was nothing more comforting than being needed. Vanity of thought kept telling me to admire the beauty of the now, the surreal nature of the situation, when she desperately needed change. Vanity of thought clashed with the need to fix the past of a distraught not-quite-demon and propel her into the future. She stood up, straight into a single trail of concentrated rain falling off the side of the shelter. She stared up, straight into it, water flowing over her face. For a brief moment, I thought I saw a small crease at the side of her lips. She was almost smiling.

"What was it you were trying to talk about?" I asked.

"I'll tell you on the way," she replied. Her eyes turned to stare into mine. The dullness of the matte contrasted with the sheen of her wet face. Her face glowed even if she did not. Humble beginnings.

So we started our pilgrimage. Red wine ordained our mission as we drank a bottle each in the train station to lighten the weight of the world and the bags.

"Shame we don't have any cheese," she said.

"Take away the taste of the two-for-five-pound wine?"

"And bread," she added, cautiously.

"True. However, I don't think Jesus would approve if he knew his blood had depreciated in value in such a harsh way. Most people get a cup of tea and a biscuit for their blood. I'm sure he was expecting more than a fiver before tax," I retorted.

She sighed, enigmatically. We started walking out of the train station. The soft orange light from the lamps overhead slowly spilled its cavalcade of monochrome. Everything was black or orange or a subtle shade in between. Even the rain poured orange, a downpour of soft, slow particles of light interspersing the black backdrop. As soon as we reached Stokes Croft, she started talking to herself.

"I used to do a lot of work around here. There's a church right next door to a hostel for the homeless. There were always so many needy people here. I was always stopped from helping them directly. Instead I had to sit there and listen to each one of their anguished cries. Mostly they made no sense; even angels can't decipher slurred idiots rambling about the pain of how life dealt them a bum card. They never realise they can try and turn it around. I guess they were the hardest ones to listen to because you just wanted to shake them around a bit and tell them to stop bitching.

"I knew angels on war detail. They had it tougher than I did. The poor folk they had to deal with had it worse than the folk I had to help, but it didn't stop it being any less brutal. I guess that's one of the problems. I know that I and they don't deserve to feel upset for things we feel are beyond our control when there's so much going on in other people's lives that actually *is* beyond their control. Yet we still feel bad, and we feel worse for allowing ourselves to feel bad, like we're being totally self-indulgent.

"There are so many atrocities in the world, but for some

reason they're only important if they're happening to us. It's worse being an angel because we're supposed to be entirely selfless. I guess hanging around you people has made me a little jaded towards the lack of intricacies that there are up in heaven." I decided it would be best to let her ramble on for as long as needed.

"I spoke to God about this a few times. I asked Him why it was that we felt this way. Why we were all seemingly built with some innate selfishness. He didn't answer. He never answered. Even though I was stood in front of Him, He didn't answer. And people ask why He doesn't answer their prayers. Guess that's what you get when you're God. You don't need to reply when you don't wear sandals." I looked quizzically at her. "I mean, if He's walking on something uncomfortable, He'll just change the ground to sand. You don't need sandals and you sure don't need to answer the prayers of selfish people. We can create worlds in our heads but we are too selfish to deal with the problems of now. We can allow ourselves to live entirely in a fantasy land where these things never happened. I guess even He suffered from that."

"Should an angel be blaspheming so much? I guess this is what you tried to talk to Him about but couldn't find the words?" I replied. I couldn't help but feel shocked by this outburst. Questions of theology were always playing on my mind, but not to the extent where you could dismiss God because He didn't wear sandals. "So what does God look like?" I asked, trying to change the subject a little.

"Whatever He feels like," she replied bitterly. She looked to the ground. I didn't know what to say. Thankfully she said it all for me.

"I loved Him."

We walked in silence until the end of Jamaica Street.

"I loved Him emotionally, physically, spiritually, agape. I would have done anything for Him but He never seemed to notice the little things I'd do. He just kept living His life as though nothing had changed when it had. I tried to talk about it but He was enigmatic as usual, probably laughed about it with his mates in the pub. I always thought Michael was a bad influence on Him. At least Raphael had the good grace to admit his mistakes." Her bile was spilling out in spits and spews. Her tears of anguish seemed to turn to tears of rage, anger at the neglect, at the loss of a love. This blurring of religious blasphemy was taking its toll. I took out another couple of bottles of red wine and offered one to her.

"Thanks," she said, taking the bottle. "Sorry about that. I just get so angry. I don't know what I'm doing and I don't fully understand what I'm saying. Sorry."

"It's Okay," I replied. As much as I wanted to tell her, I had heard the same words usher forth from my own mouth at one point. The loss of my love and the angel's loss of her love was everything to us. My love was my God. I wanted to tell her that I knew how much it hurt to be ignored by the person you revered above all things. I wanted to tell her that it would never be all right but it gets easier. I wanted her to know that she could still do remarkable things without completely destroying herself because of one man. I wanted her to know, but words failed to create and impart the feeling. Instead, we carried on walking in silence.

The city, sadly, does sleep. When it hits three or four in the morning the clubbers, the drunkards, the police are either in bed, passed out, making another cup of tea or getting into a fight somewhere other than the inner depths. There are no twenty-four-hour amenities, only lights, wind and rain. As we walked, huddled into ourselves to keep any warmth we had, we stumbled over old memories. It was as if we had walked this way before. The beauty of Cabot Tower, perched on a green hilltop in the distance, reminded her of a time she had stood up there on New Year's Eve and watched the horizon explode around her, ushering in new possibilities. The waterfront reminded her of people she had had to take care of, or people crying solemnly at being alone in a group of strangers they once called friends. The docks reminded her of the beauty of the sunset. The city reminded her of all the good she had done.

The rain had done its job; it had washed away some of the pain of crying, the cathartic walk releasing the memories of better times. Still she seemed only to forget to remember the things that could happen, only paying service to what was. We sat down on a jetty on the docks.

"I remember this. You brought me here before we split up," she said.

All this time I was mistaken. It was me who was the drunk. The lights from Clifton and Lower Clifton (as the inhabitants like to call it) flickered serenely on the water, playfully shifting into a myriad of shapes and forms. I could feel my exhausted mind make patterns from the static on the surface of the water. The only sound I could hear was her breath and the gentle lapping of water as the rain slowly broke the surface, becoming the whole it once was.

"This was the last time I loved," I replied, solemnly. "Does this mean you're not staying?" I asked, suddenly feeling alone and incomplete. My mind was creating all sorts of images in the water, anything that would remind me of her. Anything so I didn't have to let this moment pass. It had created her in front of me, a character from a former play, the last memories of her. I knew that all she had said was because I had wanted to be reminded. Reminded of how badly I had treated her and how crushed I was when she did the same to me. They were all my words. I had just wanted to hear them from her, so I made her up for this one, drink-fuelled night.

"I was your angel. It's time to let me go. Who else can I rely on? Let's let all the memories go when everything can be perfect one last time, even if it isn't real. If these are your words, I can change you. For this is what I have decided for myself, not to come to you again in sadness. For if I make you sad, who is there to cheer me except the one that is made sad by me?"

"Two Corinthians?" I replied. She smiled, and her eyes suddenly lit up with an incandescent blue. They released me from my waking nightmare. She turned away.

"You don't have to remember any more." Her wings spread wide, angled into an arc above the redemptive angel. She left me for the last time. She left me with no more imaginings of wholeness, no more invented fantasies. She left a drunk on a jetty, smiling. Fearful of the future but knowing that, finally, there could be one.

A Blue Tale

Rachel Bentham

And if the crash comes?

I expect to meet you in the rubble,

half a brick in hand.

Here's mine.

Together we can build a crack.

Philip Gross

Greg said it, quietly, in the kitchen, almost under his breath. *"Je t'aime..."* He meant her to hear. Lotte was peeling onions, dropping them into a huge bowl, lots of little pickling onions. She'd got a sack of them cheap, and they pricked at her eyes but she held her head up, away from the sharp reek of them, fighting the desire to cry. His self-indulgence was infuriating – how pretentious, saying it in French. She answered in English, her hands still stripping off thin, brown skins, regardless.

"Well I don't." Gruff. He had a bloody cheek – she did have a boyfriend, after all. Greg sat quietly at the kitchen table, eyes lowered. He had a talent for silence, but Lotte wasn't about to crack. She'd heard him talking to the plummy women who phoned him, his tone similarly wistful. It was what he did. She could feel hot shoots beginning to creep up her neck, so she grabbed the boiling kettle and doused the onions. Blanching, it was called in the preserving book. Nothing more was said.

Steam mushroomed up to the ancient, stained ceiling. It was a shared house; huge, cheap and rotting. Although it was as unkempt as a student house, none of them were students; they were older, probably wackier. The house contained Greg the cave diver, Alastair, who worked in the natural history part of the museum, Cath the teacher, and Lotte, who was an artist. It was like an old farmhouse, but not a farmhouse, with thick stone walls, freezing in the winter, dim and cool in the summer. All around the house spread roads lined with tidy thirties semis that had sprung up after the war. The owners had gone abroad, and left their family home gently dilapidating, marooned in urban sprawl. There was an exhausted piano in the hall, which sometimes tinkled at night. They put it down to mice. Wetsuits and oxygen tanks hung in the old walk-in larder. The fridge was half full of grass snakes and drowsy adders in plastic ice cream boxes, while spiders and butterflies in film canisters filled the egg and dairy sections in the door. Alastair went on collecting missions in the hills between Bristol and Bath, searching for adders under stones in the early mornings, finding spiders in Bickley woods out past Conham. He kept them in the fridge because the cold slowed them down into something like hibernation.

He'd take them out into the garden, helpless and immobile, and arrange them – butterflies perched on flowers, snakes carefully curled among rocks, too cold to do anything but let themselves be positioned for Alastair's camera. He entered the resulting pictures for wildlife photography competitions, and sold them to natural history magazines. Good for his career. How wild is a chilled butterfly? Alastair said he adored wildlife. He would get quite agitated talking about a mosquito's mouthparts; his eyes sparkled and he began to gesticulate enthusiastically. As a child, he'd made cardboard masks of insect heads. He secretly brought a black widow spider back from abroad, hidden in his camera bag. After he'd done the fridge treatment and photographed it, he released it in the garden. The great British garden spiders ate it, much to his amusement.

Lotte grew weed and a few vegetables in the overgrown back garden. In the daytime she took Greg's bearded collie for long walks, through the allotments, to St Werburghs city farm, along the railway tracks, up to the Downs, out along the Frome valley at Stapleton – miles of paths and pavements beside a crazy, leaping heap of grey spaghetti. She knew all the green places in the city, and sometimes on her walks she found pieces of wood that she carried, or dragged, home. Her bedroom was strewn with wood, and things she was making. The lampshade was made of twisted ivy, and a small dead tree was a lamp. Sometimes she and her boyfriend went exploring at night, watching a badger snuffling along a footpath beside the Cut down at Temple Meads, or sitting under a hawthorn watching the stars over the Avon Gorge.

Lotte was recovering her strength – she had just come back from dying. Her skin was paper white, her eyes were clouded a deep, deep turquoise. She had been so ill she had almost given in, drifting in and out of consciousness, travelling into the bliss of white space. But, at the last ditch, she had decided to let death go instead; decided she had things to do, although nothing would have been easier than to drift away. She had been to the place most people were most scared of, had a good look at it, and let it go. For the time being. So nothing fazed her. Her deep blue eyes had a relentless gaze. Her boyfriend, Mack, came and growled at the others in the house, at their excesses of middle-class enthusiasm. He was earthy, solid, unforthcoming. Lotte was increasingly fed up with him. He believed she could save him from his own generally miserable state of being through the power of love. She doubted it.

She told Greg about Klein, her current inspiration; he was the artist who made International Klein Blue – canvases covered solely and solidly with bright, intense blue. The hottest, most cloudless sky, heavy enough to weigh on your chest until you were breathing blue, pure and clean as the air racing through a seabird's lungs. Above the ultimate, most azure ocean. Or the bluest of eyes. She found it hard to explain in words. Sometimes she painted blue eyes onto her wooden constructions, chinks of blue peeping from the knots. For her, blue was spirit, a colour you could fall into and happily drown.

Greg's voice was soft and cautious. To Lotte, it felt like watching a cat licking its smooth coat, knowing how the tongue would grate on her own skin. Much of the time, she felt like he was trying to impress her. Trying to impress never cut any ice with Lotte. Greg and his cave diver friends would gather to loudly relive their underground, underwater close calls; fondly recalling the crawls, the tricky bends, the muddy sumps they had dived through, holding their breath, with no oxygen tanks and barely room to squeeze their manly shoulders through the tight gaps in the rock. They laughed about the mud they had trailed into the pub where they downed their real ale; how wild they looked; oh, they were so mad... There were seemingly endless conversations about bits of equipment – clips and valves, the best glue for wetsuit seams. Drinking beer and being their own heroes. Nothing wrong with that.

Lotte went caving, sometimes. A gang of them bumping out to the Mendips in an old van, changing into overalls and hard hats in a twilit field, some of them grabbing a last fag beside the muddy entrance. Then, one by one, they disappeared into an unassuming hole in the ground. She so relished slipping into the not warm and not cold insides of the earth, groping at rock damp as a new baby's head. Sliding and twisting her body through bellying tunnels; downwards and sideways and upwards until all sense of direction was distorted and all that was left was wriggling in dark holes in the ungiving innards, refusing to be scared, trusting to the sheer force of her own body, her own confidence. And she relied on the others' knowledge of the caves, their odd, notional maps, spare batteries and advice about equipment. Glad to be with them. Once, there was a lone bat, deep underground, fluttering through the haze in the roof of the cavern in which they were resting, smoking. They didn't know if it was lost. She knew cave diving was even more intense – adding the incredible claustrophobia of underwater; masks and tanks, the dark water holding the cold of elsewhere.

Greg's eyes were blue, but pale. In response to her talk of Klein, Greg showed Lotte photographs of the Blue Holes, where he had dived in the Bahamas, colourful spreads in the Sunday supplements. Gorgeous aerial photographs of sapphire sea, splotched with the wobbly circles of far deeper blues, the holes disappearing down through the ocean floor.

Insets of Greg himself, and a full-page glamour shot of him in snazzy yellow diving gear, his head torch illuminating a striped fish. He tried to be casual – the Holes were what mattered; he ignored his own image as if it was irrelevant, while his talk of the beauty of the underwater caves ran close beside Lotte's ear, smooth as a strong current. But Lotte knew. She knew what he wanted to be – a hero. She knew that he would find squeals of admiration and consternation deeply gratifying. The most she was prepared to give out was a thoughtful "hmm".

She scanned the text: '...important discoveries of hitherto unknown species...'

"Why is it important to discover a blind shrimp that no one knew was there?" she asked. "Has anyone suffered from a lack of blind shrimps...?"

She was laughing, but she remained stoically reluctant to gush over scientific discovery. Greg just laughed back. The word 'unspoilt' littered the columns, and Greg continued to talk as her eyes flicked over sentences that were presumably purpose-built to attract sponsorship. It didn't attract her. Something about it felt sad and empty. Greg was talking up the difficulties with equipment and local facilities when Lotte cut in. "So what's this about unspoilt? I don't understand...Doesn't all this coverage just encourage people to go there? And then will it be spoilt?"

He warmed to this, still smoothly purring at her side, and also moving up a notch to the greater gravitas of he who knows more. "The Blue Holes are so deep they still haven't been fully explored," he said. "We need the sponsorship to be able to get over there. It's an incredible system. Other divers have gone so far and stopped. An American diver was lost down there, years ago, never came back. Maybe he got stuck, or disoriented, who knows? Oxygen tanks only last so long. It's completely still once you get deep enough inside the Holes, no current at all, and very poor visibility. You could barely see a yard ahead in some places. Stuff just stays down there, hanging in the water. Like the dust of ages." He shrugged.

"It was amazing, and yes, more people go there now, maybe because of the publicity. It's inevitable. Of course it's a dilemma...but they enjoy it. Don't they have a right to enjoy it, too? Do you know what? I even came across a Coke can on the last dive – it was disgusting...There's no escape from multi-nationals."

"So aren't you part of it?" said Lotte. "Aren't you contributing to that?"

Greg shrugged it off. "It's my living. There aren't that many caves to dive...It does have its downside, but since I've got the expertise...not many people can do it. Maybe it's a bit like mountains; because they're there. It's a great feeling – the best."

He sat down at the table with the colour supplements and the onions, pushed some onion skins aside and rested his elbow in the space. "I've probably gone further than anyone into the Holes, mapped out places no one else has seen. Probably. On my last trip, I got into a cavern that no one knew about. Visibility was very poor because of the detritus in the water; as I said, there's no current. When I held out my arm, I couldn't see my hand. I took hold of something that squashed between my fingers. It was the American diver's hand, held together by his wetsuit. He must have been there several years, suspended in the water along with the sediment. Nothing to disturb his body."

Except you, Lotte thought, grimly. She went back to the onions. She didn't believe in heroes, but she told Greg the photos looked good because they did. His photos won prizes. Obviously hard won. He started on about the technology necessary for underwater shots, the weight of the cameras, the need for powerful lighting. Lotte peeled, thinking about prizes, undisturbed shrimps, and the chilled wildlife in the fridge. Curls of shining onion skin piled up on the chopping board. Alastair always insisted it didn't do the creatures any harm.

As winter approached the house grew colder, clammy. The electrics fizzed ominously in the damp walls – there were reasons why the house was so cheap. The joists under the bathroom were soft, sodden – you could pull out lumps of wood like sponge and squeeze the water out of them. Filling the bath even half full seemed reckless, considering the weight on the rotten joists below...They all left before the winter set in, separated into different lives, relieved. Cath and Alastair became an item, while Lotte and Mack parted company. Lotte got her own place, and, once she'd paid off her share of the bills, the others from the house didn't come visiting.

Occasionally, Lotte heard something about Greg. More exploration of the Wookey Holes in Somerset, further dives in the Blue Holes. A record-breaking dive – fastest, deepest, through icy water, whatever. Years later she heard about Greg's last dive, somewhere off the British coast, nowhere exotic. When she heard she felt sorry. She was ironing, listening to the radio. Sorry about her so sure young self.

He had been with younger divers – maybe he had a job teaching diving, maybe it had come to that. The young divers told the story, their voices sombre and bemused. It was a routine dive; all of them had enough oxygen to return to the surface, but not enough to go further down. Greg must have known that. He was deeper than the others. Lotte could see the water – grey, not blue. He continued to swim downward, turning and gesturing for them to follow. He carried on, going deeper, not waiting. The young divers were upset, desperate – faced with a choice: risk their own lives to try and follow him, to get him to come back, or let him go.

The radio presenter's voice was as deliberately soothing as

Greg's. Lotte pictured Greg floating in the quiet deeps, fish nibbling his hair. He had beautiful hair. Or lying in the dark at the bottom of the sea, undisturbed, like the Coke can.

They saved their own lives. Below a certain depth, bodies don't float back up. Something to do with the pressure.

The Interpreter's Tale

Maithreyi Nandakumar

How little do they see what is, who frame

their hasty judgments upon that which seems.

Robert Southey

53

1. *Southmead Police Station 1pm.*
2. *Water the coriander pot.*
3. *Pizza for kids – won't forget, won't forget.*
4. *Fetch kids – 3.30.*
5. *Feed the fish – kids should have done it two days ago.*

Shoba skimmed through her 'to do' list again, written last night before falling asleep. Planning was all-important to life in this country. Shoba had been on the crest of that learning curve for a long time. Ever since she'd come to their first house – a poky terraced place in St George – ten years ago from Madras, soon after her parents had got her married to Raghav.

Ten years? Since then, they'd moved up in life, and in the city. This was a beautiful house in Redland, near the park. The area was full of beautiful old trees, Victorian houses, and a railway line that got them to nearby Bath if they felt like a day out of Bristol.

Shoba moved the chubby sandalwood idol of Ganesh in the hallway to face the right direction, and checked her appearance in the big mirror. Yes, it was as close to perfect as it gets. Shoba sighed with pride. Okay, not as good as her cousins in the States, who lived in palatial houses (in the middle of nowhere – Milwaukee, Wisconsin, shudder!), but this suited her husband and two children perfectly. Bristol was their home and she loved it. Most of the time, that is. There were times when she was attacked by an intense feeling of restlessness. Maybe she could paraglide down the fabulous Avon gorge by the suspension bridge, or cycle through Borneo for charity.

But Raghav didn't ever pay much attention to her wild fantasies. He was always practical and had a simple vision of most things in life.

"You should do something from home, like child-minding or teaching maths or science to school kids. We live in a well-off neighbourhood, there's money to be made around us," he would say, after eating the sumptuous South Indian meal Shoba cooked regularly for them.

"My son doesn't want his wife to go out and earn money. All he wants is a smiling face when he returns home from a long day's work." Shoba closed her eyes, and could hear her mother-in-law's voice in her head.

In contrast to her mother-in-law and her platoon of servants, Shoba's life as the wife of a successful professional came with the not-so-exciting duties of housework and endless cooking. She didn't need a career with Raghav climbing the corporate ladder. Doing these occasional interpreting assignments suited her life just fine, she assured herself.

She noted three new grey hairs with a pang as she put her face close to the mirror. Purpose, that's what she needed. Surely she could soon identify what hers was.

Shoba snapped the seat belt on and nudged out, waiting for a car at the other end of the road to pass through. They would have to park on both sides of this narrow road to make it extra difficult, wouldn't they? If ever there was a downside to life here, this was it.

The Southmead patrol car happened to be on the M32 when they got the call on their radio. This was the first time they'd dealt with an immigration case at their North Bristol station. Normally, it would've been Trinity Road in the inner city that would have dealt with it. The duty constables were now heading back with three refugees in the back seat, one of them a young woman.

It was the noise that was unbearable, on the hard shoulder of the M32, just outside the city centre, that cold October night. The wind was cold as they stood shivering – it made their eyes hurt. Two men and a woman – all in their early twenties, stood with their backs to the traffic. As the cars hurtled by, they felt the ground shake beneath their feet.

They'd been travelling with a lorry full of mattresses from Dover and the driver had kept yelling at them not to make themselves too comfortable.

"The lorry driver said the police will come to get us," said Muthu to his friends for the tenth time. Senthil was holding Eswari, who was throwing up from the exhaustion of the past few days.

"Thank you so much for coming." Sgt John Stevens greeted Shoba with a firm handshake and led her through dull yellow and grey corridors, to the police lockup. Inside, Shoba could only hear the noise of banging iron doors and angry shouting. She looked straight ahead; her heartbeat accelerated.

"Do you understand my Tamil?" she asked them first, her Madras accent quite different from their Sri Lankan one. They nodded their heads and smiled. Her accent reminded them of the Tamil films they watched from India. Shoba spoke to each one of them and went through the formalities with the policeman.

"Could you please tell them that they've been arrested?" the sergeant said to begin.

They were inside the prison cell.

"You've been arrested," she repeated dutifully.

And then it was made clear that the police were entitled to keep them under arrest before they sought legal advice and applied for asylum.

"Could you ask them how they arrived here?"

"In the back of a mattress lorry."

"Where were they before that?"

"We were driven onto the ship."

"Do you know where from?"

"Germany, Suisse, Afghanistan, Libya, Cyprus, Russia, and before that Colombo – we were blindfolded most of the time, so we didn't see much."

Muthu and Senthil said that they'd been targets of the many terrorist groups in Sri Lanka – people their age would get bullied every day to join the guerrilla army. They lifted their trousers to show the scars on their legs from the beatings and one of them had cigarette butts pressed on his leg. That's why their families had sold everything to send them away from all the troubles, so that they could make a normal living in another country.

"Do they have passports or any papers?"

"No."

"Did they go through an agent to come here?"

"Yes, they each paid two thousand pounds to a Russian agent – once in Colombo and again in Moscow."

All through this, Shoba noticed that the girl, Eswari, was keeping absolutely quiet, while the other two were happy to explain their situation. She was tiny with a dark brown complexion. She had long, curly black hair tied into a bushy ponytail. She was wearing a thin cardigan over her salwar-kameez, and she didn't seem affected by her present circumstances at all. Shoba looked at her directly, to see her expression.

Why did she choose this risky trip, Shoba wondered with some admiration. There was no fear when they made eye contact – no smile of acknowledgement to a fellow Tamil speaker, and a woman at that. Shoba shivered slightly, unnerved by her impassive face.

"Could you also tell them that they can have tea and coffee from the machine?"

More nodding.

"Do they have any special dietary requirements? We have chicken for dinner tonight."

That's when a look of mild surprise passed over Eswari's

face. Shoba sensed that she found this courteous hospitality most unexpected. No restrictions, they said, they could eat chicken.

She wanted to ask more questions, ask them if she'd been involved in the civil war, and was she a trained fighter? This was not the time and it wasn't her place.

Sgt Stevens escorted her out, thanking her profusely.

"So, you are not from Sri Lanka then? You speak such good English."

"Thank you, I was educated in English." She gritted her teeth as she maintained a polite expression.

"Maybe you could leave your number, so that we could contact you directly?"

His smile was too friendly, she noticed. She shook him firmly by the hand, dismissing the earlier frisson of excitement as she left the sterile, harshly lit police station.

She decided to drive out of Southmead towards the inner city into Easton to pick up some Indian groceries from St Mark's Road. And I won't forget the pizza. She kept thinking about Eswari and her courage in embarking on the kind of dangerous journey she had undertaken.

"Oh stop it," she told herself off. "War isn't glamorous. Travelling illegally isn't glamorous."

"Take me home with you – you beautiful *gurl*," cried an old Jamaican man in a suit as she slowed down on Stapleton Road. Shoba gave him a big smile and a wave and went into Bristol Sweet Mart. She always looked up to the ceiling to appreciate the art in this shop. Luscious fruit and vegetables painted with rich colours – all the more tempting to buy the real thing from the fragrant shelves.

She picked up huge bunches of mint and coriander (the supermarket pot didn't last for two days), the different dals she needed, the special raw rice from Tanjore in South India, and two bottles of pickle, baby mango and grated mango – she always bought more than she intended. At the till, she caught up with all the news of the people who ran this family business who she'd come to know well. The shop owner had just returned from a holiday to Kenya.

"I've not gone back since we were kicked out of Uganda in '72. It was an emotional journey. I came to Bristol with two pounds in my pocket," Salim told her. Shoba knew how hard they must have worked to reach this stage with this successful business, and was pleased for him.

She'd met so many people in Bristol who had such powerful stories to tell. "What's my story?" she asked herself as she turned on the heating in her car, and switched the radio onto GWR FM.

An uneventful childhood, comfortable circumstances, an arranged marriage – and even that is not half as weird as people imagine it to be. Was that it? So boring, so bland.

'Constant Craving' began to play and Shoba was moved, as ever, by its lyrics. She drove straight to the school to pick up Sudhir and Kalpana and the friend she was bringing home.

Eswari had turned into a really good cook. Okay, her food was more to a non-Brahmin taste – she tended to use a lot of garlic in everything – but they didn't mind. Even Raghav was impressed with her quiet discipline with the children. They went for walks, played board games together, taught her to say "Awright, me lover?" Shoba would see them all huddled on the sofa in the evenings when she came home from the library, giggling over the Simpsons.

Shoba and Raghav now had time to do things – they could go out to the theatre, go to London to see visiting musicians from India, and have an active cultural life again.

Her friend Clair thought she was mad to take Eswari in.

"Are you sure you can trust her?"

"It's called instinct," Shoba had replied confidently. "I can tell she is reliable and hard working, and doesn't interfere with our personal life. Once she sorts her papers and learns English, she'll be fine. She'll do well for herself."

"Charlotte seems to like her too. Is it all right for mine to come to yours tonight?" They arranged for the kids to meet up and Shoba went back to her study to work.

Shoba's management course was going really well. She was making use of the time much more effectively, thanks to having Eswari around. She still felt uncomfortable when she was given that piercing look by her. They didn't talk about her past at all. Eswari didn't answer the simplest of questions about her family, so Shoba kept their relationship businesslike. She also realised that this was different from having the kind of hired help people did back in India. There was mutual respect here, none of the usual suspicion that Indian housewives had towards the person who came in to cook and clean.

Eswari lived with them in the spare room up in the loft. Shoba had been called back by Social Services to interpret for her, and seen her sharing council accommodation with men she didn't know, and had sensed her discomfort. She seemed really bored – she didn't have anything to do all day except watch TV and go to college once a week for free English classes.

Her two friends Muthu and Senthil had been relocated to Swindon and Gloucester, and she was left behind. Shoba had hit upon the idea to bring her home. Raghav had been quite sceptical, but, six months on, they were both congratulating themselves on their decision.

"I have to leave for London tomorrow – I will be away for a couple of days." Eswari knocked on the door, popping her head through briefly.

Shoba had heard her talking on her mobile in rapid Sri

Lankan Tamil, which, truth be told, she found very hard to follow. Eswari had a network of people she kept in touch with on a regular basis. Sometimes, she heard her on the phone as she went up to bed after studying late. She must be homesick, Shoba thought, taking pity on her. And she hadn't had a weekend off in a long while now. And it was Easter weekend anyway; maybe they could do something special, just them as a family.

"Can you do some shopping for the house on the way back? The kids love okra, *vendakkai* – Indian vegetables are so much cheaper in London."

Eswari nodded her head and closed the door. Shoba thought that was a bit odd – she would normally wait for some money.

"*Na vaarain*. I will return," Eswari mumbled politely. Her backpack looked particularly heavy, as Shoba stood by the door worrying about her frail frame carrying the heavy burden.

"Go and come back carefully," Shoba called out as Eswari left to trudge to the coach station.

"It is nice to have the house to ourselves, without Eswari lurking in the corners," Raghav announced with a relieved sigh.

Shoba secretly agreed with Raghav, but wouldn't say it aloud. She twirled the glass of white wine that Raghav had poured out and admired the light that caught the crystal. It was Saturday night and the kids had gone to bed; life was good. Things were falling into place nicely, just when she'd given up all hope for her own personal future. She cuddled up against Raghav on the sofa as they settled to watch a film.

How could everything disintegrate so completely? Shoba was least prepared for what awaited her Sunday morning as she heard the news on Broadcasting House.

It had happened last night and had been all over the news while they'd been busy watching the DVD. Apparently, this lone Asian woman with a backpack had walked into a petrol station in West London and asked to see the manager, one Mr Selvadurai. There'd been a huge explosion minutes after. They were both dead.

"Oh my God, oh my God." Shoba couldn't believe what she was hearing. Raghav looked and felt shaken. Eswari, they realised, had come to this country on a mission. Her target was a man who was on the wanted list between rival Tamil factions back in Sri Lanka.

"I told you we shouldn't have trusted a Ceylonese girl. It was a girl who blew up the Indian prime minister, how could you forget?" Raghav was shouting at her.

"But Eswari didn't wear a cyanide capsule round her neck – I didn't think she'd be a terrorist."

What did all this mean for them? The phrase 'aiding and abetting' sprang to mind and they felt their heads reel in complete shock.

The police would soon be here – Shoba ran up to the loft and came back with empty boxes under the bed – parcels she'd received at this address. How had she done that? She must have taken her credit card to use it for her nefarious activity. And Shoba had respected her privacy and left her alone, had never been to her room either.

Shoba stood in the middle of the hallway and stared at the fish for a long minute – bright orange creatures slithering gracefully in the dense green of the fish tank. She could see Sgt Stevens looking stern and grim as he removed the handcuffs from his pocket to tie Shoba's wrists together behind her back. She felt a bolt of shock go through her, as she watched her kids crying helplessly.

"I wasn't expecting to see you in my lockup."

Shoba realised that life as she knew it was finished, over.

Why oh why did I ever think I was bored by it all? Why couldn't I just count my blessings and carry on the way I used to?

The doorbell went, followed by loud banging. Shoba steeled herself for the worst, with Raghav close behind her. She pulled the heavy door open with a grim expression on her face.

The black umbrella in front of her face was dripping wet. It was raining hard and she braced herself.

A carrier bag was stuck in front of her nose, thrust from under the brolly as she heard Eswari say, "You need to take the okra out and dry it on a newspaper, it will rot otherwise." She removed her trainers immediately as she walked in, touching the idol of Ganesh and pressing two fingers to her eyes – a pious gesture that came naturally to Eswari.

Shoba and Raghav were left standing by the door with the rain lashing into the house, ashamed and shocked at their own hysterical reaction. It had been so easy to jump to all those conclusions. They watched, open-mouthed, as Eswari hefted her bag from her shoulders and carried it by hand upstairs to her room.

The Daughter's Tale

Emma Edwards

This tale was inspired by a song by the band

Portishead who are a local Bristol band;

the song suggests seeing things

from a different perspective.

Emma Edwards

Children often believe in fairy tales and Mum told me many. Stories of an idyllic childhood and a youth that seemed to be cut from the pages of a style magazine. I think even she believed them. She made out Bristol to be a wonderland, where everything was bright and vibrant and all anyone ever did was laugh and dance and be in love. The photographs told a different story, pretty young things sat in the sunshine next to colourful houses that looked like childish drawings, but Mum seems to be cast in shadow, as if she was sat against a backdrop. Of course she couldn't always have been happy or she never would have left, even because of me.

The train pulls into Temple Meads station, and already I can see the rows of coloured houses, standing like children's books on a shelf, like the rows of photo albums Mum keeps on ours, and in the sunlight they seem much brighter than her faded photographs, but it doesn't make me feel closer to the truth. My father was the hero of her picture stories, this man on a pedestal, her best friend and a pillar that cast the shadow over her. But he was not hers, he belonged to someone else and so when she turned to him for comfort, after her paradise turned sour, pregnant and alone, she decided to turn herself into the martyr of her own fable, and nineteen years ago left on a train from the station I'm now arriving at.

The weather is stifling as I blink my way out of the gloom and onto the bright pavement outside. The station looks like an ornate castle in comparison to the stark boxes around it. I ask a passing stranger, laden with bags and also looking as if he's in a hurry to get away from this place, "How do I get to Clifton?"

"Number eight takes you straight up there, love," he says, pointing, with a drawl that used to be so familiar in Mum's voice but has faded now.

I thank him and make my way over to the benches near the bus stop.

I love my dad. Not my real dad, I never met him, but the dad I have always known. He's calm and honest, quite unlike Mum. He said he loved her from the second they met, and me too apparently. I remember their wedding and I was only five. It was in a church in Wilmslow and I had a cream bridesmaid dress with a gold sash, and Mum looked like a princess in ivory. She told me how Mike was the one she had always been looking for and that we would be a very happy family, and would I like a little brother or sister? I remember saying I would like a brother and she laughed. It was only a half-truth though. We were a very happy family, but I don't think Mike was really the one she was looking for. She used to describe this church near the place she went to school in Clifton and that's where she was always going to get married and it would have been perfect. I got a sister.

I need a flower for tomorrow when I visit him. There's a wooden stall painted green a little further along so I go to investigate. A man with dreadlocks and a tan is stood there and I smile at him.

"Have you any yellow roses?" I ask, without looking.

"Five pounds for a dozen, sweetheart," he replies. I only need one and I tell him so. "Well, I'm a sucker for pretty northern girls so why don't you take one?" He winks. I throw him my best smile as a thank you and take a rose. It's half open and the colour of custard. He gives me some purple paper to wrap the stem in and I walk off. Northern girl? Mum would hate that.

The bus trundles off. I'm going to stay with Becky; she lives in Clifton like Mum did. Becky and I have been friends since we started secondary school together in the flat, boring suburban town in Cheshire we grew up in. Becky always adored my mum, she thought she was exciting and bohemian and exactly like Mum wanted people to think of her, so unlike the other boring mums who had such conventional lives.

Becky loved her stories and pictures – I think that's the reason she decided to go to Bristol University. I flirted with the idea of going too and thought Mum would be keen, but she was dead against it.

"'Why?" I asked her.

"Because you'll never come back," she said in a small voice, turning away. Is that why she never went back? Because it would have been too painful to leave all over again? I always thought it was because she didn't want to see my real dad, and keep up her image of 'the one that got away'. Maybe it really was the city she was scared of.

One true thing I find out on the journey is how eclectic Bristol is. The bus passes by a large shopping area, Georgian streets, a market, parks and rivers. It is so hot and I'm feeling sensitive and vulnerable. The bus is nearly full and soon I'll have to give up the empty seat next to me. A large sweaty man, he looks Arabic or something, gets on the bus. I fold my hands tightly and shoot him an unfriendly stare, hoping that I'll somehow repel him. It works and he takes the seat behind me. A young pretty girl with a hearing aid gets on next, I relax a bit and she sits down next to me. I'm glad she's deaf, she won't try to strike up a conversation and I won't have to talk about myself. I feel bad for thinking such mean thoughts. Sometimes when I think like this I wonder about my dad. Mum may have her issues but she's so open and friendly to everyone she meets and loves talking, she would have even talked to the sweaty man. Maybe my dad was sometimes cruel to people. If I believed everything Mum said, you would have thought he wasn't capable of cruelty. But surely that means he wouldn't have turned his back on a poor pregnant friend or his child-to-be? She never gave him the choice until now, when it hardly matters. She thought more of protecting him and remaining good in his eyes than she did of me. Or is that just another mean thought?

The bus pulls up outside a large grey building. It's modern and ugly and looks wrong next to the attractive Georgian terraces around it. I know this is the right stop because I can see Becky on the steps outside. Like a negative of Mum's photos, she stands out like a beacon against the grey backdrop. I pick up my rucksack and, still clutching my rose, I get off the bus. She runs up and kisses me, shouting "Danielle!" at the top of her voice. I've been so lost in my thoughts it's hard to bring myself up to her level of excitement. I am genuinely pleased to see her though, it's been too long.

Becky talks fast as we walk back to her flat, about boys and parties and exams. She looks great. Her bright Titian red hair has grown longer and wilder since I last saw her and her frayed denim skirt and top made of green sari material seem different to the clothes she used to wear; she makes me feel drab. The thing I love about Becky is how she has never treated me different, or made an issue of my family background. Some friends have pushed the issue, assuming I must be messed up in some way. They wait for it all to come out and for me to break down about never knowing my father. But in reality nothing bad has ever happened to me. Dad, that is Mike, has been around for as long as I can remember, and really I've had as normal a life as anyone. All my family problems are history. They belong to Mum, locked in her albums and stories, and while there's no doubt she has issues to deal with, they've never really presented themselves as anything other than mild eccentricities. Even when I got the letter, it didn't seem to affect me too much, it just set the ball rolling and in a way it helped Mum get some closure, it helped her move on and let me go a bit. Becky was wonderful and treated it as nothing more than an excellent opportunity for me to come and visit. That's what I've been telling everyone, that I'm visiting an old school friend. She knows she's not the real reason I'm there but I love her for pretending.

Becky's flat is typically student with a sticky brown carpet, posters peeling off the walls and records and folders strewn over every surface. She puts the kettle on while I look round. The flat is on the top floor of one of the tall, elegant terraced houses and it makes me smile to think how different they look inside. She tells me that they're all the same – all been cut up and turned into flats. The view is breathtaking; you can see the sprawling city, the docks and the rolling countryside beyond. It's a clear evening and you can see a couple of hot air balloons in the sky. This pleases me as it adds some reality to Mum's picture; she always made out the sky here was full of balloons in summer. Becky shouts to me from the kitchen as she makes the tea, throwing options at me for the evening.

"There's a band on at the union, or we could just go out for dinner, or that club I told you about, I think some people off my course are going down."

I don't really want to go out, I'm not in the mood. It's not so much Mum's warning of how I'll get caught up in it all, and really I'm not feeling miserable, I just feel like I need to take everything in bit by bit, and prepare myself for tomorrow. I'm not nervous about going but I want a clear head. Also I did inherit Mum's habit of drinking too much at inappropriate moments and I don't want to show Becky or myself up.

"Girls' night in?" I suggest.

She comes out of the kitchen clutching two mugs, a forced smile on her face. I can see she is disappointed, she would have rather taken me out, a loud club where talking would have had to be minimal. It's going to be exhausting skirting the issue all night.

"Sure thing," she says. "I'll pop to the shops, get some wine and pizza. How about a DVD?"

It's a lovely evening. We end up with noodles and ice cream and drink a box of wine. We sit on the floor and look though Becky's albums. Us at Leeds Festival; our leavers' ball, wearing evening dresses teamed with boots and dyed black hair; the summer we went to Alton Towers with Chris and Laura; a barbecue in my back garden four summers ago; there's Becky and me, Mum, Dad, my sister Lorna, Becky's brother Jamie, back in the days when I had a crush on him. Then she gets out her new albums, the ones I haven't seen yet, of her and her new uni friends. I'm curious to see if they paint a similar picture to Mum's, but they don't. Sure, it's twenty years on, but even so, I've seen these pictures a thousand times before in my own halls of residence – student pictures, they all look the same no matter what city they're in. Except one. There's a picture of Becky with a group of friends, stood in a run-down street surrounded by people in bright costumes. You can hear the music coming from the picture. The era has changed but I've seen this picture before, it's like an echo, and for once I see the brilliance of it, the joy. I run my fingers over it.

"That was taken at St Paul's carnival last month," Becky says. "Me and Mark got so drunk that day," she goes on.

"It looks amazing," I say, and I mean it. We stay up chatting about the past and our lives now and don't talk about him. There's no point; I'm not even sure if I know anything real about him. We don't watch the DVD.

I wake up feeling groggy from the wine and the warmth. I peel myself off the futon in the sitting room and cross to the kitchen to make some coffee. My legs are shaking a bit, those skinny, bandy, pale legs; not like Mum's, which are shorter and shapely, another genetic mystery. The flat is quiet. I assume Becky and her housemate are still asleep. The clock on the kitchen wall says it's eight o'clock. I'll go now, before she wakes. I don't need a pep talk today. The cheap coffee tastes awful and I abandon it. I change into some khaki trousers and a vest top and pull my hair into a ponytail. Then I have a change of heart and brush it flat and put some make-up on – for some reason I want to look like I've made an effort. The yellow rose has been sitting overnight in a pint glass of water; I take it out and wrap it back up, and scrawl Becky a note telling her I'll text her later and slip it under a magnet on the fridge.

The bus journey back into town is a breeze. The bus isn't as crowded and I enjoy looking at the sights as I pass. Walls painted in deep indigos and Moroccan oranges seem to mesmerise me, so different to the uniform, red brick houses of our town. I see a couple of teenagers with brightly coloured dreadlocks kissing in the sunshine and young boys skateboarding. Everything in our town is quiet and somehow the people are older there. For the first time, I actually ask myself the question "How could Mum leave?" I change over to the number fifty-two when I get to the bus station. This part of the journey I know at least. I researched it well.

My heart beats fast. I've clutched the rose too tight and the thorns come through the soggy paper and into my palm. I look at my watch: it's nearly ten o'clock. The more I look out the window the less I see. Visions of Mum's photographs dance in my mind instead, all the ones that he's in. But I can't see him. I wish I'd brought one with me. I can't visualise him, he's just a grey shape, they all are, just grey shapes against a background. I don't know what he looks like and it makes me panic. I don't know what my real dad looks like and I never will.

The bus is on a wide road now, and the view of the suspension bridge is clear. I've only ever seen it on television and in books but it looks lovely. Something inside me tells me I'm nearly there so I press the button. The bus comes to a standstill and I get off. I start walking and within minutes I'm there, outside the gates of the crematorium. It doesn't take me long to find the plaque on the wall with his name on. It's at the far end. It's plain and simple and looks new and shiny. There are already flowers in the little metal container, and a photograph. The photo shows a man and a woman sat at a table in a restaurant with a beach behind. They look tanned but he still looks thin and ill. I wonder when it was taken. He has thin hair and kind eyes, eyes that don't look capable of cruelty. So now I know. The plaque simply says 'John Telford 1966-2005'. Underneath it says 'Dearly departed, loving husband, son and brother'. It doesn't say father. I put the rose in the holder with the other flowers and turn to go without looking back. It didn't say father, but then I suppose he wasn't, was he?

I sit in the sunshine by the bus stop and get out my phone. I text Becky and suggest lunch. I then press one on my speed dial. After three rings a soft Mancunian male voice answers the phone.

"Hey Dad," I say.

"Hello angel," he says, worry barely disguised in his voice, "how's things?" I tell him it's fine, everything's fine and it's lovely.

"Dad, tell Mum for me, I'm going to stay with Becky for a while." He says it's fine and Mum says it's fine. I know it is. I see the bus approach. For once, I can't wait.

A Safari Tale

Alistair Spalding

Justice is always violent to the party offending,

for every man is innocent in his own eyes.

Daniel Defoe

The morning brings a wooden floor. Suspicious white lice crawl in the dusty joins between the naked floorboards he slept upon. Rolling over does not help. The cheap blue throw/sheet has been pulled off by the tossing and turning of a rapid eye movement sleep. The dreams that kicked off the sheet quickly fade, but their essence was...hopeful. He had dreamed a hopeful dream of a new future. An 'off a friend's floor and into his own bed' dream.

Not quite the floor. The floor is for strange white lice only. He is at folded down futon level. The dirty cream squashed down futon cushion is exposing itself from under the blue throw, brazen and unashamed. It tells a tale of continual over-use and abuse, of neglect and of heavy, fat TV bums not moving for hours on end.

Eyes are weary, but rubbing them helps. He reaches for the phone alarm which, as a considerate guest, he must silence quickly. Disgusted, he realises he has almost put his groping hand into the remains of last night's dinner, not his but someone else's. The groping suddenly becomes more focused. Full attention is brought to bear on *not* putting his hand in someone else's last-night-dinner but on switching off the phone. That done, the secretive morning routines of an early-rising, considerate, futon-level guest begin. The room comes into sharp focus.

He misses the days when he would have rolled over, tucking the cover under his arm and leg, and fallen straight back to sleep, but only for a moment. That time, he reminds himself, has gone. 'Now I am a man I put away childish things' etc. For a second though, he *is* rolling back over and his arm *is* tucking the cover under itself. Then he spots a small but significant sweet and sour sauce stain and the blue throw/sheet is off. Thrown away on the floor. Then it is up off the floor and folded carefully, sweet and sour stain and all, and put away. He wants to be a considerate guest, considerate with their filth. Next, the heavy wooden thighs of the futon must be lifted gently back to its languishing squat in front of the TV.

Up. And picking his way between empty beer cans and wine bottles, over spilling ash trays and avalanches of CDs. He pulls up the blind flooding the room with bright light. Under the intensity of the morning sun, the contents of the room shrink away with guilt. The room is a backlog of filth, a monumental build-up that can never be cleared away or overcome. It can only ever be moved away from. It is a lasting testament to a student lifestyle gone on too long.

As he looks at the plates, at the stacks of old videos, at the wine glass overflowing with mould on the cluttered, dusty fireplace, he can't remember having once chosen to live like this. He heads quickly down the wooden, creaky stairs to take a shower. The house is upside down. His living/bedroom is on the top floor, the kitchen and bathroom are downstairs. He is up early so that none of the others are awake. This house has a tight shower schedule, and no cleaning plan. He is encroaching on their lives; if he doesn't wake up early enough he takes someone else's scheduled slot in the shower.

He takes a quick shower. Halfway, as he gets wet enough to make leaving the shower impossible, he realises he has forgotten his shower gel. He squeezes a small amount of someone else's Linx out onto his hand and makes it last. Hair first, then the cascading suds are used sparingly all the way down.

The towel is damp, the bathroom is damp. The steam from the shut-off shower sits there, an unwelcome guest that cannot be persuaded to leave.

There are rivers of condensation on the mirror, just as there are on the small window pane. Frantic wiping with his used, and now soaking wet, towel clears a small circle. He has left small particles of towel on the mirror. Fog obstructs his face as he tries to shave. He manages to look quite presentable.

Kitchen. Don't look at the pile of washing, don't open the fridge, don't think about how long those pans have been there. Preparation is key when being a good guest in a filthy house. Having seen the state of the kitchen the day before, he has been to ASDA. Now there is a loaf of sliced white bread and a jar of peanut butter. Two slices of bread into the toaster. Don't look at the toaster. Two and a half minutes later the toast is up, brown and just hot enough to melt the crunchy peanut butter. For a moment he closes his eyes. Peanut butter, lakes of it; ninety per cent of the toast's surface consists of melted peanut butter. The lakes shine. The taste is reminiscent of childhood. Had he ever eaten anything but peanut butter as a child? Maybe Weetabix. He could get some Weetabix from ASDA but he couldn't get milk. Milk wouldn't last two minutes in this kitchen.

The sound of another pair of legs, sleepwalking down the stairs into the bathroom, shakes him from this reverie. Don't turn around. To get to the bathroom, whoever this is must walk past the kitchen. It may be one of the girls who live here and he doesn't want to embarrass them. Wait. Footsteps go past, no pause at the door, straight on, into the bathroom. Bathroom door shuts and thin bolt slides into place. Move.

Chomping down the last of the sticky peanut butter, he considers that he must brush his teeth again. At the back, where his teeth and gums meet his tonsils, there are nuts in every gap and melted peanut butter over every tooth. He can't brush them, not now the bathroom schedule has started. A finger is not much substitute but it does its best; rooting out nuts, delving into the corner of his mouth. Hard scrubbing with finger. Hard sucking with mouth closed. Highly unsatisfactory. He sighs; this means the walk down the hill will be full of chomping on imagined peanuts and sucking at phantom butter.

Upstairs. Pulling shoes on, straightening unstraight shirt

collar. Out of the door just as he hears the first shower shift ending but before meeting the second shift runner.

Walking down from Windmill Hill. The walk is nice, but long. Through a park with a railway in it. The park has swings and graffiti, all the regular things a park should have. Melted-down bins that once contained dog dirt, streetlights that, when working, bring the shadows alive. At night the streetlights serve to highlight good places for assailants to hide. "Hide here! Look! Behind these bushes! Or stand flat against the back of this tree trunk! They'll never see you coming!" Shudder, but the night-time walk is not for some hours yet, and for now the park is friendly, the lights are off, the morning sun shines.

Under the railway bridge, past ASDA. Over more bridges into town. Here canals squirm underneath footpaths. Narrowboats chug up and down. He walks across.

Yesterday's thirty-five-minute walk to Clifton was work, today is accommodation. He has a list and a small grey folder with a push button that contains everything. Passport, National Insurance, banking details, statements from the period June '99–October '00, but nothing either side of these dates. NHS cards from long since abandoned health centres. The second pay slip from his first job. Everything he needs to feel organised.

More walking through town, a walk that will be repeated ad nauseam until he can find a place to move out into. He feels proud to be a member of these morning people. Not long ago, he wouldn't have woken up before twelve or possibly not left the house at all; he was lazy, unmotivated, adrift. Not for any reason, just because. Something happened to boost him out from post-university stagnancy, a choice was made: proactivity. That was his mantra now. Now he feels hopeful, positive about the early morning sunshine, an affinity with these other early risers. Perhaps not the people jogging, but everyone else.

Through the city centre. Half bombed and rebuilt, half eighties concrete, and in need of bombing. Tucked in amongst these halves is a thin slice of history, a forgotten doorway, an old church that you're not allowed in any more. One day these things will form the everyday, complacent scenery of his city, but for now he is a visitor and each new sight is enthralling. He senses that he has made the right choice, that Bristol is a city of opportunity. There is a buzz in the air, a successful, media, BBC-watershed-film-school buzz. People in this city are making it *all* the time. Not that he is some doe-eyed child though. He has his goals and ambitions, they are his own.

Music is playing through small cheap speakers into his ears, and he is unafraid to nod in time with his favourite pieces. Sometimes he even nods enthusiastically. People watch, and he smiles. Park Street is the hill of hills, a bike-pushing, stairlift-needed, forty-five-degree-incline hill. At the top of this is a university building; its tall tower is a memorial landmark left by an engineer called Wills. Sounds like a rich, rugby-playing, public school kind of nickname. The tower is the entrance. There is a sign up outside saying that you are not allowed in without a pass. He knows that he would only have to be inches inside of those doors to see up into the top of the tower. He doesn't have a pass but he could do it anyway. He could go in and ask about a pass and look up while they answer him. It's a tall, square tower. He wants to go inside but he doesn't.

Walking straight at first but suddenly to one side. There is no conscious decision to enter but he finds himself in a coffee shop. He buys a coffee and a toastie. He sits outside and watches the traffic. He lets his powerful early morning start tick away into a rush hour struggle, but it is worth it. The coffee cleans the last taste of peanut butter from his mouth.

He searches for houses. Each agency says the same thing. Not with their words but with their eyes. "You're a student, aren't you? Don't lie to us, you aren't a professional, are you? You can't afford this, can you? There isn't anything for you here."

The paper is more hopeful and soon he is looking at flats. Soon he will have a home.

That night he is at the house, on the re-folded futon. His sheet is now the throw again; he cannot see the sweet and sour stain. TV is on. The same plates are being reused. An attempt at washing up has been made but the general level of uncleanliness remains constant.

"How's it going?" they ask.

"Good! Here's what I'm looking at," he replies. Sheaves of papers are thrust towards them for approval.

"Hmm..." Potential flats are passed around like holiday photos.

"I like this one."

"Yeah."

"This one's cheap. I'm going to look tomorrow."

"No! I mean, no! You can't live there."

"Why not?"

"It isn't safe."

"What do you mean?"

"I'll show you tomorrow. Don't go there. It isn't safe. Look." He points it out to the others. There is a general tutting.

Next day there is a sleep-in, an agreed meet-and-tour time. Don't think about the futon, don't look at the wooden floorboards.

In the car. He sits and kicks empty packaging clutter at his feet. He enjoys being chauffeured.

"It's called the 'Frontline'."

"Sounds exciting."

"You don't know about this place at *all*?"

"No. What's to know?"

"Lock your door."

"Okay."

"And the back door. A friend was driving through and someone got in their back seat and wouldn't leave."

"... Okay."

"Don't look anyone in the eyes, okay? Just a quick drive through." A sigh. "Roll your window up."

"Okay." He is worried. "Like a safari park!" he jokes. "Don't feed the animals!" There is no response.

The drive starts uneventfully. They leave Windmill Hill but travel in the opposite-from-usual direction, away from the park, away from ASDA, away from the houses and the coffee. Within minutes the buildings are greyer, more run-down. Graffiti. Not safe, park graffiti but mean, angry graffiti. Dangerous, desperate graffiti; bored, unruly graffiti. His landlord/best-friend-with-a-room-local is the tour guide. His voice fades in and out: "Shooting here yesterday…crack house got torn down, rebuilt this bit…this is it now."

He doesn't want it to be scary, but he unconsciously checks his window and locks. He finds himself feeling happy that the car has a full tank of petrol. He doesn't want to sigh with relief that all the doors are locked, that the back doors are locked, but he does. In fact, with the car at speed, he even risks a glance upwards and outwards. He doesn't want there to be gangs roaming the streets, but there are, or at least he sees them. He doesn't want to see burnt-out cars, smashed glass and poor housing, but he does. He really wants to see one white face outside of the car so that he can sleep easier, but he doesn't.

The commentary fades back in: "Bristol…Slavery, it's all

built on it." Other words, "Ghetto, guns, drugs, black, poor."
Then the car bursts out of the neighbourhood; clean dual
carriageway takes him, unscathed, away from the smoking-
gunshot alleys and the needle-infested suicide inns.

"Can I drop you off somewhere?"

"Anywhere near the house," he says. Anywhere. But let it be
away from the images he has just seen. From the injustice and
disadvantage he is now an accomplice in, an accessory to. He
wants to be dropped off in the safe, secure, unthreatening zone
far from the noise and the dirt. When there, he will appreciate
more the smell of coffee and the relative friendliness of the
housing agent's snort. Don't stop the car until we are away
from this mess.

Later, in Clifton, is a flat, and a job, and white-lice-free
floorboards. Blue throws on the sofa and real sheets on the bed.
Sainsburys is across the road, milk is in the fridge, Weetabix in
the cupboard. Park Street's steep downward slopes put him a
world away from the ghetto. He tries to sleep and dream
hopeful dreams again.

Dreams are filled with back-car-door-entering, gun-toting
victims of old white Bristol. Filled with zombie, day-of-the-
living-dead scares. Filled with guilt and graffiti, with fear and
forgetfulness, and, where hope should be, hypocrisy.

Awake is white, Park Street-to-Redland safe, exclusive,
expensive, Fresh 'n' Wild, organic, pure. Georgian houses
stand tall and proud with rooms at the top for unpaid servants.
He now rents such a room. When they built these houses, they
laid the foundations for the safari park.

The Daydreamer's Tale

Louise Gethin

She remembers what's to become of her

as if it were yesterday.

Dave Peak

"Come on, Katie. We'll miss the train. I can't be late again," Mum says. It hurts when she pulls me down the hill, along the alley with the cobbles the men from Kerry laid, and past Graffiti Wall. She doesn't know I can see inside people's minds, their landscapes in abstract form of colour, word and smell, or that I can see images out of sight, from above and from below. Each crack and crevice of the road is filled with cement blocks mortared side by side, one on top of the other. Derelict patches of ground, where broken tile mosaics flowered with weeds are being cleared and dug for the foundations of new homes where families will grow and die. Georgian stone, Victorian brick, iron gates and the long-lost doorway covered in ivy stand side by side, watching uniformed adolescents, Asian women, men on bikes, adults with learning difficulties, a woman with a husky, overflowing bins, and yawning skips where people dump illicit waste in the quiet of the night.

Stretching down either side, the undulating cars parked on pavements stop the passage of pedestrians, forcing them to walk on the road. At the bottom, past the Cadbury House and housing association flats where the old woman who has a second-hand stall lives, a garage opens daily from nine to five; the chef of the diner acclaimed for the quality of its food smokes a cigarette on the outside steps, and a man with glazed eyes sits on the bin and begs.

In the windows of the newsagents, underneath the yellow and green signage covered in crude blue lettering, customers have pasted adverts – events, rooms for rent, babysitters, cars for sale and a notice asking for information about stolen property and requesting its return with no questions asked.

Inside, a woman in hijab picks up a tin and is discreetly told, "It's not halal." An addict folds down cardboard boxes in return for cash or cans; his pockets are searched when he leaves.

Freshly scrubbed and soft-towel-rubbed, quickstepping in front of us, a man in a suit; I think his name is…Paul. Brushing past the early morning drunk and delivery of still-warm bread, his mind's on other things: the monthly budget's due and with any luck the computers won't crash. I hear his voice in my head.

We reach the station – Montpelier, like the place in France but without the extra L or the rare elegance of the *Promenade du Peyrou*. I press the button on the intercom, which announces: "The time is nine fifteen. The next train to arrive at this station in the direction of Temple Meads will be the 9:16. The next train to arrive at this station in the direction of Severn Beach will be the nine forty-five." Birds gather opposite on a feeder. Passengers gather on the platform. Paul looks at his watch. Something unsettles me in his manner – colour dark and foreboding.

"Don't forget, I've given you money for lunch. We can't expect Auntie Sylvie to pay." When Mum gets anxious her face creases, she goes pale and her eyes disappear into the middle of her nose. I tried to copy her once in front of the mirror, but it hurt and I thought my head would implode so I stopped.

At first, a whisper on the track, then a whistle, a rattle and a deeper tone – the train arrives and comes to a halt. Expectant, we wait for the flashing yellow light illuminating the <Open> sign. Paul sees it first and presses it, causing the doors to fold in. We wait. We get on. Doors shut. Platform slides by and turns into the tunnel. Before I know it we've stopped at Stapleton Road, Lawrence Hill and Temple Meads. Mum fusses in her purse.

Auntie Sylvie is waiting at the entrance of the station with Ben. I push through the barrier. Mum waves at the others, blows me a kiss, mouths "be good", and heads back towards the stairs. Over the track, under the wrought iron frame of the roof, Paul is pacing up and down, moving his lips, his thoughts more frantic. I turn to Auntie Sylvie and smile. She went to school with Mum. They were confirmed at the same time in the church at the top of Talbot Road, liked the same boys, got married the same year and delivered me and Ben within a week of each other. Ben doesn't relate well; he's had therapy and treatment, threats and promises, kisses and smacks, but he hasn't changed.

"Hi Katie, how are you?" Auntie Sylvie greets me with a hug fragranced by Estée Lauder.

"Okay, thanks." I kiss her on the cheek.

"Say hello, Ben."

His voice rings in my head. *Hello Katie, I missed you. I've got lots to tell you.*

Auntie Sylvie ruffles his hair. "Sorry Katie, you know what he's like."

I reach for his hand. "I missed you too." Sometimes I wish other people knew what went on inside his mind – it's peculiar and comic at the same time. And he's really clever with maths, which is a mystery to me. His internal landscape is numbers and lines and graphs, his colour pale.

"I thought we could walk along the river. Maybe do a brass rubbing at St Nicholas's." Auntie Sylvie leads us out of the station down to the ferry landing designed in the shape of an amphitheatre. On the other side, Gardiner Haskins rises above the nettled lands waiting for the latest 'mixed use' development. I hold Ben's hand and feel safer than I ever feel, lulled by his whirring calculations and the archiving of stills captured by his cerebral lens. There's a rhythm resounding between us as we walk. Auntie Sylvie fills the air with observations. "Look at that boat. It wasn't here last time." A Dutch barge, bedecked with pansies, nasturtiums, French marigolds and lavender; wood-panelled inside, with soft silk furnishing; eighty feet long, fifteen feet wide. For sale.

"The water's much cleaner nowadays. I remember twenty

years ago it was filthy; one of the things that changed for the better." Auntie Sylvie puts on a brave face, but her internal colour is purple with grieving. There's not a day passes when she doesn't think of things Ben will miss.

"I wouldn't swim in it," I say, watching brown waves lap against the walled banks.

"No. But it's clean enough for birds to go fishing." She points at a cormorant that has landed on the other side and stretched its wings in the sun.

Ben's hand pulsates in mine as we pass the shot tower, old brewery buildings, medieval gate stones, the Blitz ruins of a church, spires, workers and children, men and women clinging to cans of Special Brew and each other.

Later we return to Castle Green, brass rubbings, rolled and tied with string, under our arms. Auntie Sylvie is looking for a spot. "Somewhere flat, in the sun, but with a shady bit so we don't get too warm. Here. This'll do." Just up from the footpath, overlooking the water. She takes her rucksack off. "I bought this the other day." She unzips it to reveal an inner panel with cutlery, crockery and a bottle opener. In the back compartment are the boxes of food and bottle of Shloer. "I thought we could christen it. Ben chose the colour." From the bottom, she pulls a red and yellow checked square cloth and lays it on the ground, then unpacks the food boxes, opens them and sets them down: cold chicken breast, boiled eggs, cherry tomatoes, inch-long batons of celery sticks and carrots, slices of buttered French stick and olives. Ben pours the drinks, carefully measuring each cupful so that the line is the same. I fold the serviettes and lay out the knives and forks. Above us the seagulls soar and call, swooping and dipping in and out of the water. One lands a few feet away, walks boldly towards us, eyeing with intent.

Ben's voice vibrates in my head. *We're going to France at the weekend.*

"I think that's everything." Auntie Sylvie sits cross-legged on the grass and sighs. "This is the life." She hands me the box of chicken. "Help yourself, there's plenty." She opens Ben's serviette and hands it to him. "We're going to France at the weekend."

Ben smiles into his glass and takes a mouthful.

I pile pieces of chicken onto my plate.

Auntie Sylvie's face is aglow. Purple transforms to pink. "We'll go up the Eiffel Tower. I want to show Ben all the places I visited with his dad on our honeymoon."

Ben munches on the celery sticks, evenly counting fifty with each mouthful before swallowing.

"My favourite place was the Sacré Cœur. We sat on the steps overlooking the city. We could see for miles."

After we've eaten I lie down on the grass with Ben. The ground vibrates with traffic and footsteps. Auntie Sylvie stays seated, humming, her mind skipping through the streets of Paris.

I wish you were coming. There's so much to see.

I drift off, watching the clouds; dreams blend with bells ringing, horns and Ben's calculations.

When I wake up he's staring into the sky, Auntie Sylvie is packing our things, and workers scurry along the paths back home, or stop and sit and loosen the buttons on their shirts and blouses.

"Time to go." Auntie Sylvie closes the bag. "Don't want to keep your mum waiting."

Ben sits up, blinking. *I could stay here forever with you.*

We wander back to the station. I wonder whether Mum will be happy or sad. I kiss the others goodbye, go through the barrier and sit on the bench. Paul arrives on the opposite platform; he's early, his mind calmer now, still. He scrapes his toe along the edge. The foreboding has gone. All is quiet in his mind, white. *Stand back from the edge.* In the distance, I can hear the pounding of metal on metal as a through train approaches. *Stand back from the edge.* Roaring, a red blur speeds past, drumming the tracks, pulsating the air. Paul fades to a pinpoint. I close my eyes, feeling dazed and confused.

"How was your day?" It's Mum, standing in front of me holding out her arms. "We'd better hurry!"

The Tale of Gregory Garland

Hayley Birch

...in my fancy...I climbed a thousand times

to that tall hill they call the Spy-glass,

and from the top enjoyed the most

wonderful and changing prospects.

R L Stevenson

Fifteen people in a post office queue and Gregory Garland only needs one second class stamp. The kind of characters this queue is composed of are the kind Gregory feels unjustifiably sorry for. The girl at the front with the dreadlocks he recognises as the same unfortunate soul who hands him a free newspaper each morning in the freezing rain. Just ahead of him stands a large man wearing a tattered sweater covered in white paint, and just joining him at the back is a woman with a pair of yellow tinted glasses and a prominent scar on her neck. Gregory does not know why he feels for these people; he just does, and it makes him sad. This is why he waits patiently at the back for his one stamp, tapping his foot only slightly when he forgets himself.

At the market, Gregory spies the cookie man through the bustling crowd and smiles sympathetically. As he pays for his three sesame seed cookies, he wonders at the man's remarkably good humour, which, as he sees it, there can be no logical reason for. The cookie man is shabbily dressed and unevenly shaven, and Gregory thinks he looks like he has been up since four o'clock baking cookies. In the time Gregory spends choosing and buying his three, at least the same number are eaten by passers-by idly tasting the free samples. Gregory feels his frustration.

Much of Gregory's afternoon is spent in this manner each day. He only works in the mornings now and this gives him plenty of time to pace the streets of Bristol feeling sad about all the different people he sees. Some days he thinks his heart feels very heavy with the weight of everyone else's disappointment. For him, each and every face hides a story and this story is invariably sad. A woman with a pram and dark circles under her eyes is depressed because she has all the time in the world for her children and none for herself. A girl with protruding hip bones has an eating disorder; how thin she is, how distressing. A man with a dozen tattoos is compensating for his insecurities with macho images.

On this particular Wednesday, Gregory is so weighed down by his heavy heart that he can take no more. Between Corn Street and King Street three people have already provoked a feeling of despair in him – this is above average for a Wednesday. He must lose himself in make-believe for a few hours.

So here I am, he thinks finally, when he has bought his ticket and found his seat and is waiting for the curtain to rise. Here I am, sitting in an audience full of lonely people. He begins to feel sorry for the lady to his left who is feverishly turning her ticket into confetti. But because he is keen to forget his heavy heart just for the afternoon, Gregory concentrates very hard on his bag of pink and white marshmallows and waits for the play to begin. Much to his surprise he is soon enthralled. Perched on the edge of a creaky, uncomfortable seat, he barely moves for the duration of the first act. The lonely people fidget and rattle sweet wrappers close by, but Gregory is fixated, not by the story, or by the brilliance of the acting, but by the girl.

She is exquisite. Mysterious and alluring; she tells everything and reveals nothing. She creates a warm presence but gives a cool response. She is barefoot and penniless, but Gregory does not know how to feel sorry for her – she is too wild, too ambiguous. Here is a character he wishes he could meet. If only she were real. But his regret is in the same moment overcome by her inexplicable beauty. She is not voluptuous; neither is she elegant. Helena, as the pirates holler at her in the play, is waif-like, but her dark eyes are fierce and her movements deft and strong. Gregory studies her every turn. Whilst she is on stage he can look only at her, even when she stands idle as the two leading characters fight to the death. There is something so enigmatic, so indefinable about this girl that Gregory thinks he would gladly give up everything just to meet her.

After the play, Gregory sits quietly for a while as the lonely people file out. For a second or two he is on his own with the silence they have left him. The theatre is static. This handsome old theatre, so long a centre of the city's life, is merely a finely decorated box. Gregory ponders whether time would stand still were no one ever to return. Nothing real would change here, dust would settle, that is all. No, it is not much without the people, he thinks, even the lonely people. But oh, if everyone were as vibrant and beautiful as Helena, then they would be blessed.

Later he buys coffee at a place overlooking the docks. On the opposite side of the river people are battling their way towards the bridge in the gusting wind. Gregory's focus finds a lady of about eighty, who has put down her loaded plastic shopping bag on the dock and appears to be hunting for something in her numerous pockets. Just then, as if carried on some warm current of air, Helena breezes past. Gregory immediately loses sight of the frail old woman and sees only Helena pressed against the bar. His vision shifts from weak, old and needy to fresh, young and fortunate. She is dressed exactly as in the play, save for the addition of a pair of flimsy-looking shoes and a long brown overcoat. Her skirt picks up dust from the floor and as she reaches to pay the barman Gregory recognises the same array of intricately designed bangles he has noticed earlier.

Gregory doesn't feel especially confident as he approaches Helena's table, but he has always made a point of not feeling sorry for himself and his ordinary appearance. Not very sorry. No, Gregory only feels sorry for other people, not himself. In any case, he is too dazzled by her shining skin and radiant smile to think of his wonky chin. Carefully, he puts down his latté and proceeds to pour out a stream of praise for her performance. Helena, silent, but not as if she is really listening, only smiles knowingly.

"Can I get you anything else...?"

"It's Helena."

Gregory looks momentarily confused.

"Is it?" he says eventually.

Helena explains politely that she really is the daughter of Bristol's most notorious smuggler, and Gregory's head spins. Of course, her father is getting on a bit these days, and hasn't brought home much loot recently, she admits, but they do well enough. She points out his boat with the skull and cross bones, but all Gregory can see is a flaking old barge.

Helena twists and twines Gregory's truth. She delights in distorting every idea he has about his safe and very dull surroundings. No, Helena is not an actor, she is a pirate's daughter. She has sailed to Papua New Guinea, to Peru, to the Ivory Coast. She can smell seaweed drying on the flats when she closes her eyes. Her father and his crew unload gin and tobacco at the docks in the dead of night. Helena deals in silver. Helena orders rum in the afternoon. She tells stories of swordfights and lost treasures; plundering and skulduggery. The modern harbourside with its fashionable bars and eateries is transformed into the dark, moody scene of a host of ill deeds. Gregory stays quiet until he is quite, quite sure that she is quite, quite mad, and that, worst of all, he is *desperately* sorry for her. He is in awe at her delusion and feels pained to have discovered it all. If they had never happened to have crossed paths after the theatre, or if, as usual, he had not had enough confidence about him to talk to the poor girl, he would never have known. Now his perfect notion is spoilt and the world is only sad again.

And then there is nothing for it but to be blunt – this girl is clearly disturbed. In her head she is living in an entirely different century, in an entirely different city that exists only in a bygone era. Has she no concept of cars and supermarkets and cinemas? Doesn't she take a train to work? What about her beloved Old Vic; the lights, the speakers, and the audience with their jeans and fashion haircuts and mobile phones? All this he puts to her, but Helena is not disconcerted. The city is ever-changing she admits, but it is always the same – bustling, dirty, colourful, full of life, full of all sorts of people. Gregory watches her closely as she talks. Helena does not act as if she has lost her mind. She talks with such confidence that he wants to believe her every word. Her eyes do not stray from his and she does not fidget. "It is the people who make the city," she says, "and the people who change it for themselves."

Gregory resolves to cure this girl. What a gross oversight of nature to install such a troubled mind in such a pretty head. He cannot let Helena live another minute with this warped view of her existence, and looks around for some way of proving her wrong. Presently though, he is lost for evidence. A curious calm seems to have descended and although he stares hard at the bridge, not a single car passes. Ordinarily he could sit in this very spot and watch the impatient office workers beginning to escape in their bubble cars about this time, silently cursing pedestrians and sighing at their watches. In frustration he turns in his seat to scrutinise the other customers, but he can find nothing conspicuous enough about them. A man with a squashed nose rolls a cigarette, whilst listening to his red-faced friend telling a joke about an Irishman. Three gossiping women huddle around a collection of empty glasses. One obsessively pushes her hair behind her ears, another absent-mindedly taps the glasses with a large brass key.

They are at the market. Gregory thinks he will find something to make his point here, but it is all fresh fish and vegetables and still-hot crusty bread today. The smell of home-made soup mingles with that of farmhouse cheese and just-baked fruit loaf. Helena inspects and exclaims at everything. She darts from stall to stall, skirts billowing, jewels jangling, eyes sparkling. Barnacled mussels look too good to eat, dirt-dusted carrots and asparagus delicious to her. She buys nothing but loves everything, and for a while Gregory forgets his resolution, so entranced is he.

When they reach the cookie man, Gregory finally comes out of his daze.

"Afternoon Helena," he greets her, and hands over a giant oatmeal-and-raisin without hesitating.

"You know each other?" Gregory asks, immediately filled with jealousy and intrigue.

Of course he knows Helena. Why, she is old Jack's girl.

"Helena tells me her father is a smuggler," scoffs Gregory.

"Ah, a pirate if ever I knew one," grins the cookie man, unfazed. "A real scallywag is Jack."

But she *must* be mad, she must.

Helena's enthusiasm is inspiring, her energy exhausting. Gregory's world is soon so filled with her presence that he sees and hears little else. The sad people around him flicker in and out like old cine film.

Finally, upon reaching the bar at The Llandoger Trow, which Helena refers to curiously as 'The Old Spy-glass', Gregory sees the stooping, weather-worn landlord and waits patiently. But Helena sees the sun-baked old sea dog and immediately shouts her order. With a twinkle in his eye he charges her three pieces of silver. Gregory is too exhausted to argue and follows her to an outside bench. After the cookie man he made several attempts to obliterate Helena's fantasy but all in vain. Either he had lost his train of thought or been distracted by some whim of Helena's, or the wind had changed or something, but he hadn't quite managed to pin her down. They must have passed a hundred things he could have pounced upon. Why hadn't he confronted her with traffic lights or cash machines or a shop window full of computers? Something about Helena makes him forget himself. She creates her own city, and its horizons are broader; its colours are crimson and amber and chocolate, not blue and grey like in Gregory's. People in Helena's city are full of unexpected stories. They drink and dance and joke, and they are never sad.

As they drain their glasses – she has ordered dark rum for each of them – Helena asks to hear about Gregory Garland, about Gregory's home, Gregory's family. Does he have a dog, does he like painting? What has Gregory read lately? Gregory's home is very plain, very ordinary. Gregory's family are all dead or yet to be born. He doesn't have a dog and he can't paint. Well, he concedes, no, he hasn't tried. Gregory doesn't really read much. Helena looks all of a sudden very sad and concentrates very hard on her rum.

Something shifts in Gregory's brain.

He exchanges glances with a man at the neighbouring bench. He leans back and catches hold of the table to steady himself. Helena is getting up as if in slow motion, but Gregory is thinking about something else. Realising his coat has fallen to the ground, he turns to pick it up and his eyes fill with tears.

She is gone.

The man at the neighbouring bench looks over in the midst of a loud burst of laughter at the expense of one of his friends who has knocked over his pint. The man moves away from the table in his wheelchair. Gregory feels strangely empty.

The cookie man is vague. Gregory is faintly annoyed by his cheerfulness, which is genuine, as it always has been. No, he does not really remember whether he has seen Helena today, or yesterday, or any other day for that matter. He is far too busy to notice what anyone else is doing. As for the city, it is as it ever was – ever-changing. It is not defined by cars or shops. King Street and Queen Square and College Green are empty spaces; a city is people. People who open up space to every possibility, seeing from the same viewpoint a thousand different horizons. All the people Gregory sees now are ambiguous. Faces hide stories he can't wait to hear, and everyone he speaks to extends the city's boundaries a little bit further. Although not everyone is as vibrant and beautiful as Helena, Gregory does not very often feel sorry; if he does it is usually only for himself.

A Rainy Day Tale

Laurajayne Friedlander

Today it has rained like people
Thin and newly alive
Then thick, heavy and old
The water came down like places
A drizzle of beaches
A deluge of mountains
A flash flood of far away
It has been wet like feelings
A thunderstorm of hurt
A cloudburst of ache
Torrential memories.

Laurajayne Friedlander

103

Today it has rained like people, Suzanne thought, as she stared through the window thinking of how the rain had been thin and light in the morning and now had settled to an old heavy downpour. The pavement in front of the house looked bleak. Six-thirty and almost dark. It was a filthy night to be trying to get home from work. She grabbed the curtains and pulled them tight.

"You're watching Points West with Chris Vacher and Amanda Parr. 'I want that one' and it seems everyone wants *Little Britain*. Tonight on the programme we will be talking to David Walliams and Matt Lucas, the Bristol-based creators of the award-winning series, and asking them if the larger-than-life characters portrayed in the series are based on real Bristolians that they have known."

The phone rang.

Suzanne laid her knife and fork on the plate and lifted the tray off her lap.

"Hi Mum. Oh, fine. No, nothing much, just watching the news. I'm going to watch *Casualty*. I taped it the other night. Haven't had a chance to see it yet. No, he's still at the college. Yeah, he's got these auditions coming up with the kids, you know, he said he'd give them a bit of help.

"No, Mum, I told you, the kids; the auditions for *Casualty*. I've no idea what time he'll be home, but you know Mark, loves his job."

Mum interrupted. "You know, Suzanne, sometimes I wonder if it's you or that flippin' college he's married to. If he's not down there at Filton, he's at home marking stuff. He's always knackered. It's a wonder you have any life together."

"Mum, don't go on. He'll be fine."

There was a bang on the door. It jolted Suzanne out of sleep. At first she thought it was the TV. "Blast, I'll have to rewind it, I missed the end." She looked at the fuzzy snow on the screen. The tape had finished ages ago and Suzanne felt stiff from sleeping curled on the sofa.

Another bang on the door. This time louder and sounding quite frantic.

The clock on the video said ten fifty-four. Where was Mark? He was often late but never this late. Why was he banging on the door? His house keys were with his car keys and he must have driven home, so why couldn't he get in?

As Suzanne walked into the hallway she could make out strange outlines behind the frosted glass of the front door. Blurred colours, yellow, green, and a crackly voice – a police radio.

There was a big lump of fear in her throat, like phlegm that wouldn't come up or go down. Her heart was huge in her chest; it was thumping, trying to get out through her ribs. Her palms were hot and slippery with instant sweat. Not Mark, not her beautiful, precious Mark.

Suzanne pulled open the front door. It seemed to weigh tonnes.

The policeman and woman both looked calm and sensible. The policewoman extended her arm and guided Suzanne back into the living room. She explained in her best policewoman's voice that there had been an accident and that Suzanne needed to come to the hospital. She told Suzanne to get her shoes and coat – it was very wet out, and she picked Suzanne's handbag up from the floor when Suzanne panicked at not being able to find it.

The crash had happened in Gipsy Patch Lane, near that awful bridge. Mark had only just left Filton College. The drama students were so excited about their auditions for *Casualty*. Some of their excitement had rubbed off on Mark. Later he would joke that he hadn't got as far as Stoker's pub, his regular stopping-off point on the way home.

The police officers were from Staplehill police station because they were nearest to where Suzanne and Mark lived in Downend. On the way to Frenchay hospital they reluctantly gave Suzanne details of the accident, because Suzanne demanded to know, but they only had a vague picture themselves and Suzanne knew they were missing out the worst bits.

They dropped her off at A&E and the policewoman, who was called Sarah, came in with Suzanne but then she had to go because they had another shout.

Suzanne gave her name to reception and then had to wait.

The words that the police officers had said to Suzanne began to form images that stuck in her brain and hurt like stone chips from the roadside, digging in. The young guy who collided with Mark was only seventeen, driving his mother's Vauxhall Nova. The police said they would not have believed that a Vauxhall Nova could do so much damage. He was driving so fast that his car actually ploughed into Mark's and then carried on over the top, flattening it, and landed twenty feet behind. The young lad had only passed his test three months before. He had a broken leg.

Suzanne tried to imagine Mark's car. The car they argued about because he called it 'baby' more than he ever called her. For all that they argued about it, they had had a lot of fun in it. And of course Mark was a member of the Owners' Club. "You name it, in Bristol there is a club for it," he'd told her when they first met, and it was true. Bristolians loved their clubs and there did seem to be a club for every possible interest.

She imagined his car, his beautiful Opel Manta Berlinetta 1.8s, white with body kit, spoiler, tinted windows, all that expense, now lying in a tangled heap, the panels distorted even more by the flashing lights of ambulances, fire engines and recovery vehicles.

Mark's head went through the sunroof. The staff at Frenchay told Suzanne that the fact that the sunroof gave way and smashed had saved his life. Just.

Mark had thirty-nine broken bones. Both legs, tib and fib, a bone in his arm had snapped and the spear of it had shot out through his elbow. She saw that when they let her see him briefly in A&E before they wheeled him away down a corridor and left her standing behind two rubber and perspex doors that closed with a hard slap.

Suzanne watched people come in and out of Casualty. Two drunks and a guy with a split lip. There was a child who was climbing over the seats and seemed to have very little wrong with him. Then a nurse came and said she had found her a quieter place. It was a little room off the corridor. The sort of room where you would break bad news, thought Suzanne as she sat down on the functional-looking sofa. There were some magazines on a little table and an out-of-date *Evening Post* with headlines about another Bristol City Council dilemma and some story about First Bus. The usual stuff. On the floor there was a discarded 'in-house' paper. Suzanne could make out half a headline about proposed developments for the Frenchay site.

She stood up and walked to the black window. The rain went on.

Don't leave me Mark. Don't you dare leave me now. I'll do anything. Just stay alive. One minute auditioning kids to act all this. Now it was for real.

Broken scapula, broken jaw, both cheekbones, fractured skull, possible bleeding into the brain, massive internal bruising certainly and haemorrhaging likely. Mark would need an exploratory operation, not often done these days what with scans and all that, but necessary in his case. Plus operations to set bones; some would require pins and wires and then extensive plastic surgery to his face, probably several operations.

The head injuries were the biggest cause of concern. He was being taken to intensive care. The first forty-eight hours would be crucial. Suzanne could visit whenever she wanted. The nurses reassured Suzanne with well-rehearsed platitudes. He was in the best place. Frenchay specialised in head injuries. They would do everything they could.

Suzanne surprised herself that she had held it together for three days. Daily life was measured in lists and things to be ticked off. Things to be measured and counted. Seconds and minutes.

She got herself organised. Started a routine of getting up and getting to Frenchay, became an instant expert on bus timetables and routes. With her mum's help she remembered to eat. Each day she walked down the long lemon corridor that led to Intensive Care.

Mum phoned AXA where Suzanne worked at Stoke Gifford and explained the situation. They were very good about it and told Suzanne to stay in touch and take as long as she needed. That was a relief. Mum kept telling her to "Keep your strength up, you won't be any use to him if you don't look after yourself." She did go on a bit.

Mum told Suzanne that Mark was a lovely lad, she was so fond of him, he was like the son she never had. She was great, she wanted to know every detail about the accident, about his injuries; she told Suzanne that she needed to talk about how she felt. It was unhealthy for people to bottle things up. So Suzanne told her some of it, but not everything.

Suzanne did not tell her mum that she hardly recognised Mark in that hospital bed. When Mum said he was such a good-looking lad, Suzanne hugged her for the first time in ages. She was trying not to cry. She certainly couldn't tell her mum that he had forty-three stitches in his face.

On the fourth morning, the hospital called to say that Mark had regained consciousness and was asking for her. His 'obs' were much better and he would probably be moved to a ward later that day. She could come in and visit at any time. She told the nurse to tell Mark she was on her way.

She scalded her hand trying to pour a cup of tea and switch

the radio on at the same time. GWR were playing a song by Massive Attack and Suzanne collapsed onto a chair and sobbed her heart out in sheer frustration mixed with relief. The Massive Attack song went on. She had burned her hand; it really hurt but Mark was going to be okay! Remembering what huge fans she and Mark had been, going to concerts at Colston Hall, buying every album, memorising the lyrics. Massive Attack and Portishead. Who needed Oasis and U2? She would look out some of the albums later. Play them again if she could face it.

When Mark came home from the hospital, he still had both legs and one arm in plaster. In his free hand he carried a white plastic bag full of pills and potions and Suzanne had to remember what went where and how often.

There was no way that he could get upstairs and so she made him as comfortable as possible on the sofa, telling him that because he had demanded to come home so early, this was going to have to be his bed for the foreseeable future. For nine weeks she slept on the floor in the lounge, getting up at least twice every night to help him to the downstairs loo or give him extra painkillers.

Sometimes she would hear Mark crying in the night. She could only tell when he sniffed loudly. There was no catch of breath, no sob, but when she knelt beside him on the sofa, she could see by the light of the streetlamps through the curtains, the lines of tears running down over his temples and into his hair and ears.

She tried to hold his hand, stroke his chest, gently now, so anxious not to hurt him, not sure which parts of him were safe to touch.

He would try to pull himself up and ask for a drink, so they would sit in the dark drinking Chivas Regal. Forget the expense. Forget the medication. Mark said it was better than Voltarol, Ponstan, Distalgesic, but maybe not as good as morphine.

At night-time he worried. Worried that he couldn't make love to her. Worried that the trauma would make him impotent. He had heard that it could. Worried that he wouldn't father children. "It's just a guy thing," she told him. Doctors told him everything would be fine. It would all just take time.

In the dark, the two of them talked for a long time. He was wretched, he was pissed off, he wanted to go to the pub. He could not bear to live like this! He screamed at her. He was exhausted, but he couldn't sleep. He was scared of flashbacks and nightmares. He told her to leave him more than once. Told her to find a real man. He would try to push her away with his good arm. On those nights when he cried she would kneel beside him and crane her neck to put her head on his pillow. She would cup her hand against his cheek, stroke his hair, call him baby, kiss him gently, his face and jaw still hurt.

Suzanne wanted to love him so much. She wanted to pleasure him, but he said, "No, absolutely not." He said it wouldn't be fair, anything like that had to be mutual, though sometimes he would let her slip his hand underneath the cover to touch him, stroke him slowly. He never resisted. Maybe he felt soothed. Gently the co–codamol would move in on him and he would drift off to sleep.

Sometimes in the dark she would cry. What if he never made love to her again? What if he was impotent? Suzanne desperately wanted his child when the time was right. "It's just a girl thing," she said to herself in the dark. She was wretched, she was pissed off, she wanted to go to the pub, she was exhausted. She couldn't sleep, she was scared of flashbacks and nightmares.

Mark was off work for six months and Suzanne took a lot of time off work to nurse him. They lived off his personal accident insurance topped up with benefits. It was a struggle to pay the mortgage but somehow they managed. They had some really bad days and some good days. They became film buffs, watching every new video that came out, Suzanne sitting on the floor with her back to the sofa, Mark twisting the rope of her hair in the fingers of his good hand. Their GP came round once or twice, then the community nurse and then Pam the occupational therapist from Yate. She was nice. Suzanne's mum came round a lot, and Mark's mum too, and the two of them got on really well and started going shopping together, causing a good deal of concern between the two fathers. The mums watched videos with Suzanne and Mark and took turns to cook meals and sit with Mark while Suzanne went to the shops.

They even had one or two parties when Mark's mates from work came round and they watched football on TV. There were cards and letters from the college, from staff and the students. Two of the students had been given small parts in forthcoming episodes of *Casualty* and several others had been placed on the books. All the students were thrilled and said they could not wait for Mark to come back to work. People from the car club came round and commiserated with him over the demise of the Opel Manta.

The insurance for the car came through and Suzanne bought another one. An Astra estate. Boring, but practical and economical and useful for Mark's wheelchair and all those trips to outpatients.

They had fewer bad days and more good days. Some things happened quite quickly. They soon worked out how to make love whilst Mark was still flat on his back on the sofa. He said it was the best pain relief ever. They still laugh about it, and still do it like that sometimes, and Mark will make a crass comment like, "Thanks for the memories". The pair of them will roll around on the bed or on the floor, collapsing into laughter.

Other things took more time. Mark was still on crutches when he went back to work, part time at first and too soon,

Suzanne thought, but he was determined, and desperate to see 'his kids' as he called the students. He still had faint scars on his face from the last of the plastic surgery. He still needed painkillers. Mark's tutor group had all become *Little Britain* fanatics and had him laughing with their Vicky Pollard impressions and constant banter of, "Yeah but, no but, yeah" along with, "I want that one."

Suzanne thought she wouldn't know what to do with herself when Mark went back to the college. She was sick with worry in those early days. But now she is quite happy at home. The 'mums' come round quite a lot and help out.

Sometimes she and Mark have a quiet time and listen to Massive Attack albums or Portishead. Suzanne will dance round the kitchen bouncing their new baby boy Marcus on her hip.

Suzanne's mum will come round on Saturday nights to babysit while Suzanne and Mark go to the pub. "Off you go," she'll say to them. "I'm quite happy to stay here. I'll make a nice cup of tea and watch *Casualty*."

A Tale of Discovery

Jane Taylor

An untitled poem about children playing outdoors

by James S Constant captures the essence

of this story.

It was after nine and the office was filling with chatter and the hum of computers. Yet Rebecca, who'd been there since eight-thirty, found herself uncharacteristically lost in the words on the postcard. Nicola always sent them to her work address and rarely wrote anything on the back. She liked this one more than most because she felt she could understand it. It reminded her of the trial flight of the gigantic A380 she'd seen on television the day before. The engineers on the ground looking up, heads tilted back, shading their eyes from the glare of the sun, expectant as children. She had felt a tingling all over her body and the reactions of the engineers had sparked an emotion in her that she couldn't name. It overwhelmed her and spilled out in tears which ran freely down her cheeks.

"Rebecca." A familiar sharp, clipped voice interrupted her thoughts. "Have you finished those letters I gave you yesterday?" She stood up, touching her hair self-consciously and feeling a familiar knot growing in her sternum. She moved around the side of the desk to the tray with her boss's name on, her small frame graceful and perfectly proportioned.

"I put them in here before I left last night," she said politely, making a conscious effort for eye contact. As her boss took them, she leaned in close, so Rebecca could smell the stale coffee on her breath and feel warm air on her cheek.

"Make sure you wear the right underwear with a light-coloured skirt. Or you might give the wrong impression," she whispered. Rebecca felt her face getting hotter and knew it would be turning a dark purply-red. Several people had come into the office just moments before. Excellent timing. They pretended not to hear, but it's amazing how loud a whisper can be. Only Hazel looked at her with sympathetic eyes.

Rebecca sat for a few minutes, sorting some mail. She tried not to, but she must have touched her hair a dozen times. She went to the toilets, looked in the mirror and saw that her face had gone red and blotchy. This wasn't the first time, but today it looked worse than usual. Locking herself in the cubicle, she put the lid down and sat on the toilet, which was unusually high. At only five foot two, her feet didn't touch the floor and in the reflection on the shiny, plastic door, she looked like a child. The knot in her sternum was turning to pain. Bending over, it felt a little better. She looked at her watch. Twenty past nine. She breathed in deeply, closed her eyes and let out a huge sigh. For months now, she'd been half living, alternately bored and anxious at work, depending on what mood her boss was in. At home, she watched too much reality TV, which was amusing at times but was ultimately unsatisfying, like eating too many sweets. Rebecca rarely took time off work, but she simply couldn't face another day of uninspiring administrative tasks punctuated by cryptic remarks from her boss. She called Hazel on her mobile and told her she wasn't feeling well.

Rebecca walked the short distance from the office to College Green, glad the spitting rain of the morning had stopped. The cathedral stood, beautiful yet understated, beckoning her as it often did after work or in her lunch hour. These large quiet spaces, where the slightest sound would echo, calmed her, even though she wasn't sure about God. She liked being where she knew exactly what was expected of her, where there would be no surprises. She sat on a chair at the back and breathed in deeply, closing her eyes. The smell of the cathedral was damp and musty, reminding her of the school science block, where she'd felt most at home.

Rebecca had loved all three sciences, but she hadn't been able to take them separately because a new curriculum was introduced. Her teachers tried to push her, but the exams and tests were unchallenging and had meant a bigger knowledge gap between GCSEs and A levels. She could have done better, of that she was sure, but her mother's innate belief, which transcended words, had somehow seeped into Rebecca's brain and infected her.

Rebecca's mother had kept her children's toys in separate boxes and made it quite clear that Thomas's transformers, trains, cars and Lego were out of bounds. Rebecca's own toys bored her. Barbie didn't *do* anything. Thomas had been given a model aeroplane for his tenth birthday that actually flew, high in the sky, until he left it in the middle of the driveway. Rebecca had felt a lump in her throat as she gathered the bits of metal together that had made up the engine. She had sat in her room for hours with a book from the library, fitting it back together and figuring out which part was the crankshaft and which was the con rod, and how the fuel-air mixture was ignited to provide power. She knew it would never fly again.

Rebecca stared up at the arches of stone that met a little unsymmetrically in the centre of the cathedral ceiling. They looked far away yet close. She felt tiny and unimportant, and longed for an ounce of the faith of the cathedral architects and builders, who must have believed that such a creation was worthy of their time, and that they were capable and worthy of creating it.

Outside, the sky was still grey. Park Street was a harder climb than usual and she was glad when she neared the top and saw Napiers on the other side of the street. She had never gone in for alternative medicines, associating them rather unfairly with dreadlocks, piercings, rainbow colours and people who smelt. Her friend, Nicola, used them regularly though, and had given her something when she was nervous before an interview, some kind of remedy that you put on your tongue. It tasted like brandy and she had no idea what was in it. She had insisted it wouldn't work and had taken it out of both desperation and a desire to prove her friend wrong. It had worked, but created only a minor scar on her scepticism. Today though, Rebecca hoped, without justification, that just going in the shop would make her feel better. She crossed the road and almost walked into the advertising board, which read:

We can help with:
Depression
Insomnia
Anxiety
Eczema
Allergies
Irritable Bowel Syndrome
…and many other disorders.

Rebecca wondered if her own personal disorder had a name. Beneath that, it said:

Also LiFE COACHING with Barbara Williams.
See inside for details.
Free 15 minute consultation!!!

Rebecca hated to see a small 'i' where it should be a capital. She also hated the incorrect use of apostrophes, the lack of comma usage and poor grammar in general, all of which made her an excellent secretary. She browsed the shelves, looking at the ingredients in a shampoo that cost eleven pounds seventy-five. It promised to be 'an organic experience' and to 'rinse the chemical damage caused by exposure to regular shampoos from your hair, while providing a layer of nature's own most effective protector (provided by snails without any damage being caused to them)'. Rebecca found herself smiling at this and decided to buy it for Nicola.

At the till, she stood behind a fussy woman in her late thirties, who was asking a lot of questions. Rebecca was still debating asking about the tongue drops. When she realised it was going to be a while, she began to look at the leaflets in the rack by the stairs. There it was again, 'LiFE COACHING'. As she read the leaflet, it was as if someone was speaking to her:

'May I ask you a question?' it began. 'If you were to look back on your life right now, would you have achieved any of your life's ambitions? Do you enjoy what you do at the moment, or are you just treading water until a better time? Life coaching can help with all areas of your life, including career development and change, confidence building, finding a direction and purpose...' Rebecca could feel her face getting hot for the second time that day. It was as if someone was watching her. She looked up but there was no one. How was 'LiFE COACHING' any different to counselling? She didn't like the idea of that. She scanned the rest of the leaflet in which clients' testimonials included phrases like, 'tremendously positive effect', 'fired with ambition', 'direction and purpose' and 'fresh start'. Rebecca was unconvinced but in her heart she hoped for their sake it was true.

"Can I help you there?" The voice was kind with a strong lilt of West Country. Rebecca jumped, putting her hand to her chest. She looked up to see a plump face and mischievous eyes, through stylish red-rimmed glasses. She was in her forties, which immediately put Rebecca at ease. Anyone in this age bracket was generally safe, less likely to judge or compete. "Sorry love, I didn't mean to make you jump."

"No, no, I'm fine." Rebecca's left hand went to her hair and she pushed a lock awkwardly behind her ear. It wouldn't stay when her head was bent so low, and immediately it flopped in front of her eye.

"Did you want any help?" asked the lady.

"No, I'm just looking," Rebecca replied quickly, staring at the leaflet.

"Well, I'll be downstairs if you do. I haven't got any clients for the next half-hour." Her nerves had prevented Rebecca from putting two and two together, so it was only when she turned the leaflet over and saw the same smiling face that she realised who the woman was.

It seemed like a long time to Rebecca that she had been standing there before she concluded that she had nothing to lose. Having made up her mind, she felt the rhythmic beat of her heart grow faster and harder, as if the organ was actually banging on her ribcage, fighting to get out. Before she could change her mind, she went over to the stairs that led downwards to Barbara Williams.

At the bottom of the stairs, Rebecca saw a toilet directly in front of her and a moving slice of Barbara Williams in the room to the left, as the door was slightly open. She was humming to herself and swaying on a rocking chair. Rebecca's curiosity for this odd lady was raised enough for her to forget her fear for the nanoseconds it took for her to decide, move and plant a knock on the door.

"Come in." Her cheerful voice was loud and penetrating inside the small room. Rebecca opened the door and felt calmer immediately – only a little, but enough to help her legs move. The room had a warm orange glow. Small mirrors rimmed with pebbles and paintings in vibrant colours hung on the walls. Barbara Williams motioned to a comfortable blue chair.

"Would you like to sit down? Can I get you some tea?" asked Barbara.

"Um, yes, please," replied Rebecca. Her throat felt dry. Barbara handed her the tea, a herbal concoction that smelt nice but was a dark yellow colour.

"So, what can I do for you? I see you've read the leaflet." Rebecca took a sip of her tea, which wasn't like anything she'd tasted before.

"Yes. There should be a capital 'I' in 'LiFE'."

"You're right. I went mad when I got it back from the printers, but they were going to charge me all over again to re-print them and in the end I decided to put up with it. Don't like it though." There was a silence while Barbara sipped her tea. She made a face.

"I'm not that keen on camomile. I prefer a traditional brew myself." She paused, giving Rebecca room to speak. "Is there anything else interesting in the leaflet?"

"Yes. I suppose. People say you're great. I mean, amazing," Rebecca replied. Barbara laughed. "That's just a few of the people who know me," she said. "Not all would say that. But those people in the leaflet, they should really get the credit. They did a lot of work to get to where they did. I always tell my clients, it's ninety per cent the client and ten per cent me." The beating in Rebecca's chest was subsiding.

"I supposed I could use some help..."

"What kind of help?" asked Barbara.

"Well, no one at work seems to like me," Rebecca answered, knowing that wasn't quite true.

"Let's unpack that. Who in particular?"

"Well, my boss."

"I see. How does she show this?"

"Um...she makes comments in front of people, personal comments...about my clothes...and sometimes she criticises my work in front of my colleagues when really there's nothing wrong." Rebecca could tell Barbara was listening carefully.

"Right. Anything else?"

"Er...yes. She called me into her office and told me I was taking too many breaks, which I wasn't. And she tried to rewrite my job description so I had to go down a grade."

"Tell me," said Barbara, leaning forward, "how long has this bullying been going on?" Rebecca was quiet as she processed the idea that she was being bullied. "Because that's what we're talking about here. Workplace bullying. It's more common than you might think. I'll give you a web address." She paused. "So, how old is this woman?"

"She's a few years older than me, I think."

"And is she attractive?" Rebecca didn't know what to say. She didn't want to sound mean, but the answer was simple. She was heavily overweight and carried most of it around her waste and back, so her bra strap would dig in, creating bulging pockets of flap at the sides of her back. "Shall I take that as a 'no', then?"

"Well...she is quite...fat."

"So, she's probably jealous of you. Has that ever crossed your mind?"

"No. I just thought she didn't like me."

"Is she good at her job?" Barbara asked.

"I...er...I haven't found her to be very good. She passes a lot of her work to me. And her spelling isn't very good."

"So, is it possible she feels threatened by you?" asked Barbara.

"I don't know. I've never thought about it."

"Okay. Now, let's find out what else is going on. I've got a few minutes before my next client." The only time she'd mentioned what her boss was like to Nicola, she'd tried to suggest the same thing, but Rebecca had dismissed it. She thought Nicola was just trying to make her feel better.

"So, do you like your job?" asked Barbara.

"Um, no. Well it's okay." She felt ungrateful. Barbara waited for her to continue. "It's boring actually. I'm an admin assistant. I never wanted to be an admin assistant."

"No? What did you want to be?"

"An aeronautical engineer." Rebecca surprised herself with her reply. She hadn't told anyone her ambition since she'd been at school and talked to the career advisor. "I love aeroplanes. I'd love to work on engine design."

"Well, you're in the right city. So, what's stopping you?"

"I didn't get very good grades in my A levels. My mother didn't want me to go through clearing. She said the university wouldn't be very good. She didn't want me to do engineering at all really."

"I see. But what about *you*? What do *you* want?" Barbara's factual manner of questioning forced Rebecca to think quickly, and to speak before her hesitant mind had a chance to claw back the answer.

"I want to go to university and study engineering. Mechanical. It's what I've always wanted."

"Gosh," said Barbara, sitting back in her rocking chair and laughing. "If all my clients were like you, I'd be out of a job. So, you know *what* you want. We just have to figure out how to get you there." Rebecca was comforted by the simplicity of Barbara's logic.

"Would you like to come for an appointment next week?"

Barbara asked, opening her diary. Rebecca hesitated. She didn't like using her credit card.

"I don't get paid until the following week," she said, "and er, I'm not sure…"

"If it's the cost, you don't need to worry. Did you see on the back of the leaflet? I have a sliding scale. And you can spread the cost."

"Oh. Well then, yes."

"What day suits you?" They fixed a time a week from that day and Barbara gave Rebecca a list of questions to think about and some websites to look at. Rebecca went upstairs and paid for the shampoo. Outside, the sun had begun to shine through the slight cracks in the clouds and she was grateful for the warmth on her face. She walked up Berkeley Avenue to Brandon Park, noticing that the tiredness in her legs had lessened, and in her stomach, she felt something different. She climbed up Cabot Tower with an ease she hadn't felt since childhood, and stood at the top, looking over the city for a long time, watching planes pass overhead and dreaming the dreams she had locked away for years.

The Tale of
Juma the Rich

Polly Carr

The city is a place of continual motion

where things form and disperse

connecting and separating

the language you speak

may not be the one I understand best.

Fiona Hamilton

Juma arrives in Bristol as workers are leaving their offices and heading home, or to the pub or to meetings. He sees that the pavements and roads are busy with people and traffic. Busy and noisy. At first, standing still in the middle of all this, he feels he doesn't exist or only exists as a statue, like the ones he can see up on platforms around the centre of town. The taxi driver who has helped him with his bags (well, you would – a fare all the way from Heathrow, a bit of chat about football, and a tip that will keep him in beer for a week) gets back into the cab, but, having watched his fare standing in the street, looking a bit overwhelmed, he buzzes the window down and

"Well, mate, this is Bristol, this is the centre – where was it you wanted? I can take you if you like; I'm good at finding me way round…"

"No my friend, I will walk. I will walk and find it. My legs are tired from all the sitting. I will ask and I will find it. I thank you nicely. I mind you." That wasn't all Juma said, it was followed by something that the driver figured was Swahili and sounded like a prayer, a blessing and an invocation all in one. But the driver, feeling ashamed of his ignorance of other languages and other cultures – as well as a deeper shame, that of turning his back on the god his mother had loved – ducked his head back into the cab and pulled out into the traffic. A parting cheery wave and he was gone.

Juma breathes in and out and in and out. He is uncertain what to do next, but feels pleased to be here and pleased to be standing up, out of the taxi. It's the first time he's been in a taxi that he hasn't been driving himself. This thought makes him smile – a slow, wide smile. He's come so far and things have changed so much. He looks up at the front of the building where there are pictures of people dancing and smiling and the word 'FAME' in big letters. Back home there is a cinema and he thinks it may be a cinema building. The pictures of people smiling make him smile some more. Off to one side, he can see the harbour and there are some fountains on the ground, although most of them are not working. There's a man nearby shouting "Issue, Issue!" and holding out a magazine. Juma approaches him and takes one from his hand. He opens his mouth to ask for directions and

"Pound twenty, please gov, and bless you for buying it," says the man, his grin showing some gaps and his face showing some wear and tear as he looks into Juma's eyes. It's a little while before Juma understands that a transaction is taking place; that something is expected of him in return. He thought you had to buy things in shops in England, but gradually he realises what to do and takes a note from his pocket. He thinks it is ten pounds. He knows better than to haggle, which he would always do back home. "Well now, gov, I don't have that kinda change on me 'cos that would be asking for it. Lemme nip into Boots and get them to change it for us." And the man disappears into a shop. Juma has heard the words and could repeat them but he's not sure what they meant, not all of them anyway. He thinks many thoughts very quickly. That the man is a thief and he must pray for his soul. That the man is very hungry and has taken his money to buy food. That he, Juma, did not understand the price of the magazine or that the man was afraid he would be caught selling on the street and has run to hide from the authorities. He picks up his bags and starts walking along the road and up a hill. He chooses this direction because almost every other way would mean going across a road and there are too many cars moving too fast. He will feel better if he walks a bit, and now a girl in not enough clothing is handing him a piece of brightly coloured card. He sees that her hands are stained with ink from the cards. He tries to look away from her body and tries to calculate how much money he needs to give her, even though he's pretty sure he doesn't want the card and

"Gov, here, wait up, you don't have to give her money for that, 's just a promo piece, a flyer. Here's your change, sorry man, I was as quick as I could be." Juma turns and a jumble of coins is presented to him. For a moment, he now thinks he should give the magazine back, but he stops himself just in time and instead he puts the coins in his pocket and holds out his hand to shake. He knows the English shake hands – he's been told it's their way of saying hello, praise God, bless you, how are you? How are your family? Peace be with you and your wife and your children, goodbye – and anything else they need to say on greeting or parting. He knows you can make a deal with a handshake. The man grins again and shakes Juma's hand firmly and

"Hey man, you've done some graft in your time," he says, turning Juma's palm to the sky. "And there's me thinking you was just another of these rich African tourists we've heard about, come to see the sights and spend your caffeine fortunes. Not that we see many of you round here – I mean it's not Bath or London or Shakespeare country here you know. Just a bit of a tatty harbour, lots of pubs and lots of kiddies that don't know they're born. What brings you here, anyway?" Juma understands he's being asked a question. He understands the man admires him but he doesn't know why, so he asks his question, the one he has had ready in his head for four years.

"Please tell me the way to Jenni's home, which way do I go?"

128

The man looks a little baffled, but Juma also thinks he must have made a joke because the man is smiling, and before he speaks again a laugh comes out and

"What? You telling me you've come here and you don't know where you're going? Who's this Jenny? Ain't you got her address? Oh man, I don't believe this. Don't she know you're coming?"

All these questions make Juma crestfallen. He feels idiotic and out of place. He *is* idiotic and out of place. He is just beginning to worry that he won't find Jenni so easily. In Stonetown it would be a matter of moments before someone knew who he was talking about, whoever it was. Even with common names like Mohammed, people could work out who you wanted by a little description. But all the same, maybe he should have e-mailed her to say he was coming. But that would have spoiled the surprise.

"Jenni. With 'i' at the end. She is a sugar trader. She was my boss. She is kind lady and sent money for my wife when our first baby was born and each since. Now I want to visit her to stay in her house and help fix her garden, for repay. She have hair from a bottle and favour red lip paint. She kindest lady I know not from Unguja. Now you show me how the way, please." Suddenly very tired, Juma feels tears coming to his eyes. Since he bought his computer he has sent pictures of the babies and Jenni sends pictures of her garden and her friends. He has brought her Yassi's paintings to go on her fridge and a clay cow made by Hammed who also used to work for her before he went to study art in Dar. His cows now sell for big sums and he will be very famous soon. Jenni will be able to sell the cow if she needs money in a hurry. He wants to help her in her garden, he wants to talk more with her; they always had such good talks using bits of Portuguese, bits of Swahili and bits of English. And he wants to find a house to buy so he can bring his children here and see if he can get them to a good school. But all his hopes and dreams, all his riches and joy are lost to him in this moment. He wants to see his friend and he can't find how to.

Juma notices the promo piece, flyer girl laughing at him. She rolls her eyes at the man who sold him the magazine; she is trying to share the joke with him. Juma can see how it is – just as he and his friends had grown up laughing at tourists in Unguja with their stupid clothes and their panicked faces and their ridiculous out-of-reach riches. And the real joke now is that Juma's money is not really his. Where can you grow coffee on Chumbe? No – it's his brother's fortune, made when all the coffee crops in Sumatra and Brazil and other places failed because of the weevils. And Tanzania's survived because no one went there any more because of Aids, so the weevils did not spread to there. And his brother who had moved to the mainland, had sent him money so he could stop digging the fields, driving a taxi for Mr Maboub, hauling sacks of grain onto a lorry, having his wife work all hours mending the sacks that split. They still worked – no one else would tend their garden – but now it was for joy. And this thought makes Juma laugh. And the magazine man laughs with him, not with the promo piece, flyer girl, and

"Well, gov, I've got to get to a meeting now, but if you come along, once we're done I'll help you find your friend. There's so many that are coming that it's an open meeting, no one will mind you being there. We're online so if you've got an e-mail address for her then Bob's your uncle. An' if we don't find her, I can get you in at the hostel." Juma thought they were called hotels and didn't realise you needed to go with someone else to get into them. But he realises that he has understood the words of most of what the man said. Although what those words mean, he's still not so sure. But not so worried, now he knows the man will help him. He shakes his hand again. He is proud to say, "I am Juma, I am from Unguja, you call it Zanzibar. I mind Liverpool. I was poor but now I am not." He is all right again – a little tentative and uncertain, but no longer afraid, or afraid he will cry, and

"I'm Mike. I'm from right here. I support Spurs, so we're enemies. But I'll help you. I'm poor, but I'm sober, thank God." The man, Mike, gives him another gappy grin. Juma's favourite smile is his family smile, the one Yassi makes him do even when he is cross with her for bossing the other children. The one he finds every time his wife comes in. Thinking of this, and hearing God mentioned, Juma feels the peace of home, of hope. No, more than hope. Faith.

They walk up the street together, talking football. They are both fluent in that. And God. Mike has plenty to say about God. Juma thought English people didn't know God but Mike does, and although his scripture, his 'Big Book' that he loves, is not the Bible, it is clearly full of God. Mike's eyes are brighter when he talks about this book and his soul shows through. Mike says that God is new for a lot of people here. He links it to having no coffee, but Juma thinks he may be making a joke about it because he's laughing as he says it. Not being able to afford coffee, Mike says, people took more to drink, and without coffee that was unbearable, so they turned to God to help them stay sober. Juma doesn't drink alcohol, he never has. But he is glad that away from home he will still be able to afford coffee, so he feels sorry for the English for these troubles. Mike says that recovery and Twelve Step programmes are everywhere now and people are in two camps, those who go to the pub and those who go to meetings.

Juma is not really sure what all this means, so Mike says it's like either you support Liverpool or you're a Spurs fan. And they laugh again. As they walk along, Mike is greeting people and hugging them and handing out cigarettes. Each person is introduced to Juma and Mike feels sure that someone will know of Jenni. But Juma is not sure. She's not a person for crowds so maybe she doesn't go to pubs, or to meetings. Maybe she doesn't support either team.

Now there is a whole crowd, like at a match, and they walk into a big building where there are more people bustling about, setting out chairs, putting cups on saucers and pouring tea from a massive pot. Mike steers Juma into a back room and they find a computer with a queue of people waiting to use it. Clearly Mike is an elder, as they all move out of his way when he says he's got an urgent message to send. Juma types in Jenni's e-mail address and 'Surprise' in the subject box. Mike gives the address of the place and Juma types quickly, ending his message with their traditional ☺ : -) – two smiles, one for each of them. Then the meeting begins and Juma is lost in all the words. He is tired but happy. He understands that all the people there are helping each other and celebrating and rejoicing in God. They tell stories of their lives and he hears the word 'surrender' over and over. Someone is celebrating their birthday and Juma is considered a special guest, so is invited to have some cake. It is delicious and sweet and on his face he feels what Jenni calls his icecream smile – that first taste when she bought him a *gelato* from the little Italian parlour she loved. It closed when the tourists all left and Jenni had been sad. And he had been sad when she left since he had never had a boss buy him ice cream before. Or talk with him so much. But now he thinks of it, they never talked much about God.

This time, as he helps her in the garden and meets all her friends, Juma vows he will talk to her about God. And, thinking of this, taking another mouthful of cake, he smiles some more.

Laura's Tale

Darren Croucher

let thy soften'd heart intensely feel

Robert Southey

Pete was listening to The White Stripes as he typed at the laptop. Rain fell against the window as the music pounded out of the Bose speakers on the shiny pine floor.

As his fingers rapidly flowed the beautiful code seamlessly across the screen, he marvelled at the perfect clarity and digital enhancement produced by his new Linn separates; the muscular, jangling guitars had never sounded better.

He paused as the raucously out-of-control song ended. With subtle sounds the new system discreetly and digitally shuffled the tracks on the CD he'd burned the night before. The insouciant drums started again.

He glanced at the Saturday *Guardian* lying open, the remains of croissants and coffee next to it on the low glass Ikea table. Laura could clean it up. He had too much to get done today: code to write, shopping to do later in Bristol. Let her do it, if she decided to actually get up this morning.

Laura was half awake yet still dreaming, her consciousness resisting the persistent music from the other side of the wall.

In the quiet between the songs she was aware of the rain on the window. She kept her eyes closed and her body curled up beneath the heavy warmth of the duvet.

A memory drifted, a feeling. Being a teenager, catching the train from Trowbridge to Bristol on cloudy Saturdays. Warm and confused images of coffee houses and shops, trains and countryside, conversations and voices, sensations, the warmth of the sheets lulling her back into dreams.

Laura opened her eyes, hearing the two-tone sound of a train's horn. Late morning lie-ins, easy days with no hurry, the sounds of trains on their way to other places. She missed her early childhood in Bristol, but she had to admit, she loved Bath on Saturdays like this.

"Morning," she shouted through at him over the music as she walked past the lounge door to the bathroom. Pete looked up to see her disappearing from view.

"Hey," he said.

She stood in front of the mirror, looking at herself closely. Pushed her hair back with both hands, held it above her head, studied her face, her neck. She let it fall.

She wandered into the lounge, carrying her coffee. She sat down in the deep sofa, sticking the coffee on a steel circular coaster on the wooden floor, the thumping music vibrating up through her feet into her body.

It was giving her a headache.

"Do we have to listen to this?"

He didn't reply.

She got up, walked out, taking her coffee through into the bedroom. She sat on the window sill, rivulets of water running down the glass, looking out over the park to the trees and the hills.

He put his head round the door.

"You need to get ready, remember, we're going to Cribbs Causeway this morning?"

Laura didn't look round.

"Yeah."

Pete hesitated there.

"Soon would be good?"

"Yes, fine, all right." Now she did turn. "Relax, okay?"

"I don't want to leave too late, you know I've got this stuff to do for work, that's – "

"For Christ's sake, I said I was going to get ready."

It was another hour before they left the house.

Laura didn't say much on the way, preferring to keep quiet and stare out the window at the countryside flashing by. Clouds in the sky. When they hit the M4 she just kept staring at Bristol in the distance, her city beneath the lines of white and grey; the city moving closer as the motorway curved round to meet it. The wipers worked harder the closer they got. The traffic grew denser and slower.

It was still raining over Cribbs Causeway when they'd finished shopping. Laura waited for Pete by the car. The parked cars reached away, grey lamp posts everywhere, the whole place long and low and stretched out towards the motorway.

Sheets of rain fell, wind whipping her face as she looked at the desolate view.

He eventually appeared, struggling with the bags.

"Can't we see a film?" she asked. She could see the cinema several car parks away.

"C'mon, let's go."

Pete slung the bags into the back seat and got in. Laura stood in the falling rain, wanting to lose herself in sensual dreams and magical light.

She sat quietly as they raced through the greyness and wetness along the busy motorway, under motorway flyovers.

Inside the flat it was gloomy. Laura sat in the front room. She didn't care what he was up to. She ate a bar of chocolate and flicked through the pages of her magazine. She turned again to the film article, lingering on the evocative images, her head full of the heady haze of the scent of chocolate, the woman's face and body, the look of her dark hair on her naked shoulders, the sexuality of the image of her in the bath, the murmur of dreams of this woman in the mirror looking away from the sadness of her reflection and seeming to murmur, "I don't know".

Pete wandered in with a coffee. He went straight over to the computer by the window and started work again.

She put the magazine to one side and looked out the window for a while. "Mind if I put some music on?" she asked eventually.

He kept typing, shook his head.

She went into the gloomy end of the room away from the window and the cold grey light, and slid a CD into the system.

Pete watched her dancing, an intent expression on her face. He watched her moving her body and wondered where she was.

She was crying a little as she danced.

Eventually she sank into the sofa, lying across it, staring past him out the window. He stared at her. He looked back at the screen. His flow was broken.

The music was more lonely than before. The day was ending in deepening gloom. She began to sing quietly. Her voice beautiful and tremulous over the messed-up beats and looping breaks. Her singing was quiet and hypnotic.

Later, she lay on the bed in the fading evening light, listening to the traffic outside.

"Hey," Pete said, quietly.

Laura opened her eyes, turned her head sleepily.

"Hey." She yawned. "I was asleep."

"Yeah. You want to do something tonight?"

She stretched out on the bed, wanting to lose herself.

"I know what we can do," she said.

In the living room, he handed her two pills.

"We used to do this every weekend," he said.

She swallowed them. "I know."

He turned off the lights. They could barely see each other. He switched on the red lamp in the shadowed corner of the large room. Dark redness all around them, their faces leering in red-clawed shadows. He kissed her. Their consciousnesses already altering. The room shifting subtly. Dissonance fragmenting the atmosphere. Dark complex beats scratching out of the speakers, unleashing themselves, flying wildly around the room. The redness full of grinning teeth and shadow-eyes and wildness. She leaped naked in the furore of erotic noise on the sofa and on the floor. Shape-shifting in and out of each other, the violence of their bodies in frenzied transformations, the apocalyptic acceleration into horror and blood, faces distorted, smiles twisted leers, shifting features rapidly moving, blurring into light, shuddering back into multiple creatures, screaming and laughing wildly. The Sony widescreen flashed multiple helicopters into the red-lit shadow-world, the abstractions of many helicopters on the move, lifting off and circling, globes of light in a geometry of movement, fear in motion, strange shadows moving across the walls, sounds chopping waves through thickening air, heavy atmospheres laden with menace, plumes of smoke, slow-motion strobes revealing horrors out of darkness. The dark red light with furious noises, a woman with long thin legs and long thin arms and long thin fingers like a spider all around her, fingers penetrating her deeply, legs bending, arms angular, snapping and biting, small teeth attacking her neck, her body, while the long legs and arms and fingers worked her all around and inside. Flames rose, blue eyes stared, the ever-present sound waves of helicopters in the wild landscape stretched out long and low in failing light, their arms around each other as they fell round and round, everything darkening around them, quieting, until there was only silence.

She woke up before him. A fragile butterfly, wings delicately bruised. She crept into the lounge and put on a new CD. She followed the voice to the window, seeing through the rain to the pale mist beyond. She let the beautiful melancholy accumulate around her until she could hardly breathe.

The CD quietly stopped; the near silence of rain falling.

Early that evening, they went to the cinema.

Thousands of red lights in a sea of shimmering skyscrapers at night, molten steel and glass, hazy dawns over densely packed cityscapes, lonely faces staring down through glass high above at the cold, empty space over Tokyo at night. The full-lipped Sofia-like beauty of the girl and the weary face of the older actor, the gentle shading of the evolution of love among futuristic Tokyo high-rises and in lonely ambient spaces, the sadness of parting. She cried at the end with the girl on the screen. She wiped her tears away so Pete wouldn't comment on them. A couple in the front row stood as the lights went up, joking with each other; the boy touched his finger to the girl's mouth as she smiled.

Laura listened to the soundtrack that evening while he worked. The poetic evocations worked subtle evolutions, her mind full of escapes. She dreamed of intense connections and the loss of future loves. She dreamed of fields of electromagnetic light in twilight. She dreamed of pale dawns barely in existence over densely packed cities. She dreamed of horizons like fire.

They made love that night.

Monday morning. She felt sad, and not very well. Laura couldn't face work, but she wanted the car, so she agreed to pick him up from Bristol that evening, once he'd finished at the office and been for a drink on the waterfront. He left the flat, leaving her still in bed. The curtains in the bedroom were drawn. She couldn't tell what kind of day it was, but the quality of light took her back into other mornings, other times. She remembered them walking around the little village near Bristol that cloudy day, exploring quiet, narrow streets, looking around the little bookshop, drinking tea in the hotel, having to cycle on through the pouring rain to her father's where they'd been staying. It had been so lovely then. She found it hard to breathe thinking about it; the intensity of something beautiful and gone tightened around her chest.

She stayed in bed until long after twelve, all tangled in hot sheets. She got up for the bathroom; she sat in there for a long time, just staring into space.

Absently Laura moved around the flat, still naked, picking up magazines, flicking through, putting them down, looking at CDs, placing them back, wandering without purpose until she found herself back in the heat beneath the tangled sheets.

She lay for a long time, the room warm and full of light.

Laura woke up with a start, looked at the clock. Already after three. She sat up, rubbed her eyes, her face. She should get ready.

Laura sat on the end of the bed. She stood up. She went to the window and drew back the curtains, warm late afternoon light flooding the room. She stood, resting her hands on the sill, staring at the trees and hills in the light. It looked lovely out there.

Ninety minutes later she was on the A4, driving into Bristol at dusk listening to the Lamb album, celestial ambience in the warm interior of the car, trees flashing past, fading orange sky beyond them.

She was aware of the glittering lights ascending the hill, the pale sky above, driving through the shining lines of traffic to the light and motion at the heart of the city.

She parked in the multi-level and walked waterside, the expanse surrounded by towers, the silver-mirrored IMAX sphere and the early evening palely beautiful, the air carrying the hush of traffic, the edges of Bristol beneath the purity of the sky.

She felt so many memories flowing with the sounds carried on the cool air, as though she were already in a future where she was alone, as though he had already faded into this cold landscape. She kept walking, to the furthest edge of the space. Across the road, through a chain-link fence, she could see a disused car park, weeds pushing up all over it, lit by pale pink lights shining through the nearly leafless trees.

Laura turned around, seeing the people walking across the far side of the concourse, a glimpse of brightly lit glass-fronted pubs, the shining bridge over the hidden water, the multi-levelled car park rising above the trees.

She waited, wondering what to do. This was where she'd grown up, and when she moved away to Bath, this was where she came back to, drinking, clubbing.

She remembered The Streets playing at the Massive Attack all-day gig in Queen Square beyond the car park the year before, how amazing and intense it had been, their last close time despite the bitter and hateful arguments before, during and after; fault lines widening irrevocably. Laura's eyes brimmed in the cold air. She wanted to hold him and she never wanted to see him again.

The event had been incredible, the mellowness of the afternoon drifting on the sweet smells of greasy food and thousands of spliffs, the beginning of evening, twenty thousand people jumping up and down to The Streets, the bellowing from the stage to make some noise. The vibe of all those people wanting to be lost in the hugeness of it all, twenty thousand lighters held aloft, and the girl with the soft red hair and shiny black top whose boyfriend had gone to get drinks. Dancing next to her, they'd brushed together, and smiled at each other. She had beautiful eyes beneath her fringe, this girl shifting her body subtly; Laura intensely imagined the taste of her, her slow kiss, being with her in her bed late at night in a flat in some distant part of Bristol. If the girl had asked her to come back to hers she just might have, yearning with the aching sadness in the swirling washes of sound over the garage beats, something epic in the air, never knowing it was over until it was too late, something amazing and sad happening. Laura couldn't stop watching this girl, hypnotised by her, wanting to hold her and breathe her in and be frantic with her, and now she was lost.

Laura could see there was still a line of fiery orange on the horizon; the west was calling her. This was the place, the moment. She started to cry again. She loved this place, but it was time to leave it.

She walked, to the bustle of the waterfront pubs, over the bridge, across the leaf-strewn ground, under the stark trees, into the lift in the car park and back to her car.

She reversed away from the sunset, drove off through the car park, the view rotating as she drove round and down, descending through the near-deserted levels, strip lights through concrete pillars, red-pink dusk behind trees seen through the spaces between levels, swinging round, down the ramp under more cold neon and concrete, pressing play on the CD now, *100th Window*, the bleeps giving way to thunderous sliding bass as she pulled out into the dense Bristol traffic.

Taking corners, smooth bass lines stepping deeply down, the dusk sky rotating across her view through the windscreen as she accelerated round, reaching speed quickly, the landscape sliding by her on her left, road veering right, fading fiery lines of the horizon moving across her left wing mirror and her rear-view mirror and her right wing mirror, pale orange and faded blue, flashes of headlights, smoothly digital notes like digital waterfalls, crushed cracked crystal ambience, ghostly voices drawn out and lingering in echoes, the clarity of the sky at this time, the beauty of the shining lines of traffic flowing beneath it.

The M32 carved its way out of Bristol, leaving the beautiful city twinkling and glittering behind Laura in the mirrors, only traffic and sky ahead; rapid skitter beats over digitalised textures and hypnotising orange and white lights blurred her onto the M4, the voice sweetly soft, a digitised angel while the sky was vast.

Racing past fields of light, lines glowing brightly, drawing their power from invisible energy flowing into them, making them shine intensely, rushing onwards to the point where the M4 swept to the left round back towards the city and the M5 emerged, reaching on towards the sky's fading glow. The music laying its shining tracks of light beyond her, its beautiful gliding tracks ahead of her into the dusk. She did not know if she would follow them but she would find out. She knew this album intimately, but she did not know where she would be when it ended. Her new world was now constantly unfurling only just ahead of her; she raced to keep up with it as the decision point approached, the motorway curving right and her path of light outstretched in front of her. She pressed her foot further down onto the accelerator.

The Caretaker's Tale

James MacVeigh

My Duties do not take up two Hours of the Day.

Thomas Chatterton

He awoke as usual before the alarm went off, and, as he stared through their bedroom window at the cliff face of flats opposite, his mind filled with its never-ending argument, vocation versus remuneration. "He's got very substantial emoluments," a gruff Yorkshire voice said inside his head, and a Norah Batty, Thora Hird voice replied, "Ee, you'd never know it to look at him!" He smiled faintly as the clock gave its pre-alarm click, quelling it with his outstretched palm before it could wake his wife and child. As he put his uniform on, he looked at their dark, sleeping heads and thought, Remuneration has to come first. Downstairs, he drank a cup of coffee and stepped out into the St Paul's Gardens council estate.

The laundries had to be unlocked by seven, and when he found a condom in the first he made a mental note to inspect it that night for working girls. Next he had to check the foyer area of a multi-storey block for urine or worse. No excremental log or loofah today, thank God, and even the lift was dry. Thinking about senna pods and the estate's latest Phantom Crapper, he walked around the side of the building to his colleagues' restroom, an Aladdin's cave of cleaning paraphernalia, dismantled vacuum cleaners and disembowelled washing machines, whose air was a blue fug of tobacco smoke. Dave Curry, the senior caretaker who had four months left to retirement and no longer gave a toss, if he ever had, grunted a greeting and the others stirred.

"Morning, everyone." After five minutes' desultory conversation he had had enough, and pointed to a newspaper cutting on the wall, 'DANGERS OF PASSIVE SMOKING', itself turning a brownish yellow though it was only a month since he had stuck it there. "I didn't give up smoking to sit here inhaling your recycled cancer." They muttered uncomfortably. "See you!"

He returned their cheesy grins brightly, knowing they

would start talking about him the moment the door closed. The job was only bearable because he usually worked alone, but his heart sank when he retraced his steps and was confronted by a great wedge of faeces, looking as forlorn as a beached whale in the very centre of the lift. As he fetched a shovel from his storeroom, he remembered social housing projects in Singapore whose elevators were fitted with sensors, so that even a whiff of bodily excretion would make the doors lock and return the lift to the ground floor where the janitor, alerted by a buzzer in his office, waited with mop and bucket to force the miscreant to clean up his own antisocial mess. Looking at the turd for only as long as it took him to lift it onto his shovel, he wondered, Am I paying the price for not living in an authoritarian state, where masturbation is illegal and the possession of chewing gum incurs a two hundred dollar fine?

He held his breath as he flipped the Richard III into one of the big steel bins that stood beneath the rubbish chutes, then went home to his wife. She was sprinkling talcum powder over their infant son's bottom like salt from a Fish 'n' Chip shop shaker, and her radiant smile brought her native city of Manila to his mind. He felt again the heat of a city that seemed in memory to be populated entirely by hungry street children and blind, limbless beggars. Knowing that this was unfair, he made himself recall the orchids that grew wild in heaps of garbage at the roadsides, and compared these to the freshness of his wife's face when they had first met. This makes it all worthwhile, he thought, living here rent-free, working on our doorstep, and still able to do my own thing.

"Eberyt'ing okay, darleeng?" his wife asked in her sing-song voice, and he could only reply, "Wonderful!"

After breakfast he sat with baby Frankie on his knee until he could put it off no longer, then he got up, picked up the dustpan and brush that were the tools of his trade, and set off on his daily round. His loved ones stood on the step to watch him go, and he had only travelled a few paces when his child's voice stopped him.

"Pankie go nursey, Daddy! Pankie go nursey!"

He looked over his shoulder and saw, with a sudden, jarring shock, his own father's Irish seaman's face staring at him through his child's Oriental features.

"Have a nice time at nursery, Frankie."

The event kept him thoughtful until he saw old Mrs Gregory emerge from her ground floor flat. With a bandana knotted over her head, she clutched a broom to her bony chest in a way that momentarily transformed the backdrop of her bog-standard 1960s council flat into a shanty town shack in Port of Spain. His heart sank as she approached, for her face sagged with a distress that was all the more real for being imaginary.

"They bin in again, Jim! When mi go to bed mi put mi bag underneat', then when mi get up this mornin' it in de kitchen!"

"Any sign of a break-in?" he humoured her. "Did you leave a window open?"

"They have a key! They make demselves a cup of tea and leave me toilet dirty!"

"Who'd do that around here, Carmen, break in and not steal? Are you sure you didn't get up during the night?"

"Yuh t'ink I'm talking nonsense?" To his relief she moved away, looking for someone else to whom she could impart her tale. "They must be mad people, yuh hear me?"

He walked ruefully between the bushes that led towards the walk-up blocks, remembering the way they had been festooned with ancient carrier bags, crisp packets and condoms when he took on the job, and admiring their neatness now. The realisation that he was taking a pride in his work made him uncomfortable as he walked through the first block picking up litter, but his discomfort was forgotten by the time he cleared a blocked rubbish chute, standing back to let accumulated garbage crash down into the empty bin below. Block one of five, done.

In the children's playground he swept up a swathe of broken glass from beneath the swings, left by the winos who sat there most nights. They were usually amiable enough, and he would not enjoy expelling them that evening. Although their behaviour could have had dire consequences, it paled to insignificance when he found two bloody syringes in the Wendy house above the slide where little Frankie loved to play. He took a container bearing the words 'CONTAMINATED SHARPS' from his pocket, dropped them into it and walked to the next block, where he pulled an overflowing wheelie bin out and put an empty one in its place. Then he climbed a graffiti-covered staircase and walked along his second landing.

"Morning, Mrs Jamal."

"Good morning, Jimbo." There was no mistaking the flirtatiousness in her manner, something he had once found surprising in a Moslem woman. Other ladies peeped from doorways along the landing, their faces veiled but their dark eyes brimming with laughter as she said, "You come to take care of me?"

"I'll unblock your chute any time you like, Mrs Jamal," he said, put off in reality by the red stains of betel nut that stained her lips and teeth. As he strode, brush in hand, to the bin room, there was a mild ululation behind him, reminding him of Palestinian funerals seen on the TV news. The bin room, a horrific sight that morning, made him stand back and mutter, "Those bloody Wedlocks!"

The majority of residents on this block were from Dhaka or Delhi, Bombay or Bangalore, but this particular mess was unmistakably Bristolian. The Wedlock family scorned the use of refuse sacks, which would have eaten into their weekly giro, preferring to empty plates and saucepans of unwanted food directly into a bin. When this was full they tipped it onto the bin room floor. Other tenants had added contributions to the heap of rotting filth, so that it sported a garnishing of cotton wool buds, their endings lacquered with brownish ear wax, while dry husks of corn cobs protruded here and there. The contents of heaped ashtrays had been peppered over the top, decorated with paper tissues used to wipe God only knew what.

Not for the first time, he reflected that an artist like Tracey Emmin could have made the Wedlocks' rubbish into an impromptu work of art, one that worked on two sensory levels, for while the sight was arresting, the stench would make the watcher nauseous. In the past he had dragged unwilling housing officers along to share the experience, and this had led to warning letters being sent to the family – he had found these in their following month's filth. Now he simply crouched on his hunkers and cleaned it up. "You're a garbage control operative," a voice said inside his head as he did so. Strangely, living with the detritus of other people's lives made him smile. If I wasn't what I am, he thought, hearing these voices would probably mean I was schizophrenic.

Mrs Jamal and her neighbours had vanished by the time he emerged. As he walked along the empty landing trying to expel the smell of the bin room from his memory, he reflected that the words 'nostalgia' and 'nostril' came from the same root, and remembered the cordite and burning wood smell of long-ago Bonfire Nights. He wondered if, in years to come, a passing whiff of garbage would spark off sentimental feelings for the present time. He doubted this as he made his body language look relaxed, and walked through the group of gun-toting, crack-dealing Yardies loitering in the doorway of block three, making it look like a seedy CD cover shot in Trenchtown. Inside, he paused for a moment to watch socially responsible tenants, the overwhelming majority, pick their way across the yellow lake that had grown overnight at the bottom of their stairs.

He fetched a mop from his secret lair, a room given over to the storage of the stereos and sofas, beds and bicycles he found and did not want, but could not bear to throw away. He mopped the stairwell slowly. When he had first started in the job, his enthusiasm had made him lunge into tasks like this as though going to war, but this had only made the rank, sour-smelling urine splash over his face and, once, into his mouth. As he made his way back to replace the mop and bucket, he recognised a familiar figure limping towards him. He stopped to chat, for as Resident Community Caretaker this, too, was part of his job.

"Okay, Turbo?" As they exchanged a ritual contact of skin he noticed that seen close up at nine o'clock, an unearthly hour here in St Paul's Gardens, Turbo Thomas's skin looked greyish. "What you been doing? DJ-ing all night?"

"Yeah, man." Turbo gave a shifty grin. Afraid perhaps that DSS spies might be lurking with the broken bottles and Aids-filled condoms in nearby bushes, he opened his hand briefly to release a glimpse of the twenty pound note he was holding. Only someone who knew Turbo well would have noticed that he was carrying his weight on one foot. As he bent to put his heavy box of vinyl reggae records down, the caretaker noticed a flash of pale pink at one ankle. He looked surprised. "What's up, Turbo, run out of black stockings?"

"I got a ladder in me last one." The two men shared a moment of humour as Turbo hitched his trouser leg up towards his knee, revealing a pink plastic artificial limb. In reality, it was a disgrace that the NHS could not match the colour of the real one he had lost in a car crash on the M32. "Have to get me lady to bring me one next time she comes over."

"Why don't you buy a pair?"

"Can't do that." Turbo shook his head, and when the caretaker noticed one or two white hairs among the black he wondered, Am I going to grow old here too? Turbo grinned. "Don't want them shop gals thinking I'm a transvestite!"

There was a pause. They watched pigeons winging their way around the buildings to swoop into the broken window of an abandoned flat. The caretaker made a mental note of its location before he asked, "Have they moved you yet?"

"Nah." Turbo shook his head. "They ain't done nuthin'."

It was crass and insensitive by any standards to allocate a maisonette where the bathroom and lavatory were upstairs to a man with one leg. The caretaker knew what labour this involved for Turbo as he asked, "Did you see them like I said?"

"No." Turbo's eyes, made red by hours of *ganja* smoking, roamed evasively along the rooftops. "Can't *you* tell them?"

"I already have. They won't do anything until you come in and complain." He caught Turbo's gaze and held it. "God helps those who help themselves, mate."

"God help me, then," Turbo said as he walked away.

He finished his remaining blocks, went home for a cup of coffee in the empty house, and came out again to do some weeding. As the only member of the caretaking team who did this without being forced, he cursed his own conscientiousness. As he did so, he noticed a paper bag caught on a high tree branch. He had seen it the day before and ignored it; now he tried to do so again, but he had to fight his upbringing. After a minute spent trying not to recall the words of a long-ago papal edict, 'A fair day's work for a fair day's pay', he brought out his litter-picker. Muttering the Dalek shriek that made his baby son laugh, "Exterminate, exterminate!" he plucked the paper bag and binned it.

By noon the area was much livelier. As people milled about, going to or from the shops, calling on one another or passing through on their way to the nearby city centre, he had a last look around to make sure everything was shipshape and, yes, Bristol fashion. He stared again at the cliff faces of the flats and reflected, not for the first time, how like boxes they were. Behind its concrete walls, each was crammed with a cargo of people from Barbados or Belfast, Mogadishu or Moldova, Tirana or Tamil Nadu, every one of them replete with a history and chock-full of hopes, dreams and ambitions. Out here on the streets, without walls to divide or protect them, they rubbed along in a mass that seemed cohesive as each sought a place in the organism of a city that had stood for more than a thousand years. St Paul's is a gateway into British life, he thought, a filter newcomers must pass through to find a place where they can belong.

After a minute he shook these thoughts from his head and went home. Inside a maisonette that was identical to those of his neighbours, he took his uniform off gratefully, washed his hands thoroughly and went upstairs. He was still on call; a tenant might appear at his front door at any moment with the news that they had locked themselves out, found a poisonous snake on a stairwell, or dropped a DVD player down a rubbish chute by mistake – all things that had happened in the past. With luck, though, he would get the peace to do what he wanted. This is the reason I was put on the planet, he thought as he sat down at his desk in front of the window and switched his computer on. He stared into space as it flashed up its series of messages and played its electronic fanfare, enjoyed a few moments of quiet thought, then centred the text and typed:

No Walls in St Paul's
by
James MacVeigh

The Immigrant's Tale

Steve Probert

She has made me half in love

with a cold climate.

Robert Southey

Rain was spitting in my face as I went to our usual meeting place, a little courtyard behind Corn Street. The crooked little space, right in the heart of Bristol, was deserted. My heart, beating so hard with anticipation, suddenly sank. I paced the glistening flagstones. This secretive yard, a place of intrigue and excitement, now seemed dark and oppressive. The buttresses of the ancient church, black with soot, glistened with the softly falling rain. Only a little row of bright red flowers, set in tubs, relieved the gloom. I circled the iron lantern, which could have come straight out of Narnia except that it was topped with energy-saving halogen lights. I checked my watch, afraid that it had stopped. The minutes slipped by and I knew she wouldn't come. She must have had a change of heart. I felt the bitter taste of rejection in my mouth as I left the courtyard, slowly, reluctantly, glancing over my shoulder to see what I couldn't yet believe.

The shower passed and I stood isolated in a sudden burst of sunshine. It was the second Friday in June and the weather was still throwing the erratic tantrums of a toddler. I stopped at the edge of the pavement, the busy office workers flowing past me like a river. I gazed at the sightseeing balloon rising high above the city, tethered by a steel cable. Katie said she loved flying. I'd hoped to tempt her, to tease more precious time from her.

The tickets I'd bought burned in my jeans pocket, a painful taunt at my presumptions. I took the balloon ride, conscious all the time of the space beside me which Katie should have been in. The day had turned out colder than expected and I was virtually alone on the flight. My head was dizzy with disappointment and I gripped the basket as though afraid of heights. The strange city spread out before me, highlighted here and there by patches of sunshine. Bristol seemed chaotic, a sprawling maze of streets, ancient architecture sprinkled with modern office blocks and water coiling around it all like a serpent. It was very different from my home city, Warsaw, but beautiful for all that. There were treasures below that made me curious. Katie could have described them to me. I had to check the urge to question the solid, empty space beside me. Her pretty smile haunted me and my heart ached. A rising sense of anxiety began to gnaw at me; a grizzled old mutt with a bone. What if something had happened to her? She might be sick or injured. Or just tired of the game, a colder voice tormented.

At five hundred feet I could see for miles. Katie was down there, lost somewhere in the bustling city. I wondered how hard it would be to find her. I had a few clues to work on but I wasn't good with puzzles; I reckon I'm just clever enough to know how stupid I am. The balloon began to sink gently back to earth, almost imperceptibly at first, as the cable drew us down. I decided to see how far I could go. I was restless after waiting around all week.

We sank lower and one of the sights, a new development circled by six giant cranes, lodged in my mind. I had no idea why, surrounded by the beauty of the older buildings, this site should hold me. I watched it until it sank from view and we landed with a grinding bump. I walked back towards Corn Street, Katie's words tumbling through my mind.

"The trail to my home starts with six great birds." Her sparkling green eyes lit with laughter as she gave me another clue.

"Six great birds?"

"Red they are in colour, just like my hair. You can't miss them." She kissed my cheek and slipped away. Robbed of her elfin beauty, I noticed the shadows and shivered in the cold courtyard. It was Tuesday and I had another empty day of my holiday left.

I stood on the corner, facing the brightly coloured stalls of the market. Beside me a street vendor displayed his selection of magic mushrooms. And like the revelation of a drug, I saw the reason for her teasing laughter. Cranes were birds. I felt a squirt of excitement, pure exhilaration as I caught her first clue, like a quickly blown kiss. I searched the busy streets, but from here the cranes were lost to me. I regretted my slowness; I should have guessed when I was on the balloon and traced a route to them. I walked through the crowded market, past stalls of CDs, retro clothing and fine craft work. If I could find my way to the centre I might have a clearer view.

I was happier moving, alternately dodging the crowds on the pavement and the cars in the narrow street. I passed an Italian restaurant, 'San Carlo' lit in bright neon in the window, a torch mounted on its heavy stone walls alive with playful yellow flames. I'd wanted to take Katie there for our first date but she'd refused. That would have been our first real date. I'd spent five minutes talking to her and knew she was the one for me.

"Meet me in All Saints Court," she said when I phoned, and stupidly I thought I'd won her. We met on the Monday and her words dashed my hopes, a glass of cold water thrown in my face.

"You can have a real date with me when you knock on my door," she said. "Until then you can have just five minutes at a time."

"That's a lot of doors, can't I have a clue?"

"I live in a beautiful little house. It might almost have been named after me." Katie tucked a lock of her cropped hair behind her ear. The boyish cut accentuated her petite beauty.

The city centre basked in sunshine. The blue sky held cannonball puffs of white cloud, whipped along by a breeze. The waters of the shallow fountains sparkled as they tumbled over the yellow steps. There was a statue of Neptune holding a trident. It reminded me of the mermaid in the Old Town Market Place at home. But she brandished a sword. Still the cranes remained hidden from view.

I walked to the waterfront and became confused by the layout of the roads. To my right a sharp bend took the rushing cars up to College Green and the University beyond. But I was sure that route headed north, away from where I thought the cranes were. I wandered down the quayside, past bars and nightclubs towards a bridge with two enormous statues in the shape of trumpets. Instead of ending in water, the quay opened out into a square filled with more statues and places of interest to explore. I found a route through to a road which ran beside the river and, as I followed it, I caught sight of the tower cranes. Two of them swung in smooth arcs, lowering slabs of concrete to feed the hungry building. The traffic here was caught in a snarl, hemmed in by roadworks. I stopped beside the works and felt my initial excitement seep away, as though carried by the slowly creeping river.

"I walk past a forest," Katie said, sipping from a styrofoam cup of latte. I'd bought the coffee for her on Wednesday, when the winds had come from the north and chilled us. I'd asked her what came after the cranes and had frowned at her reply. She gave me a cool, measuring look as though I'd revealed a temperament she didn't care for. I watched her cup empty like a glass holding precious sand. I felt an ache in my heart and knew I was falling.

There was no forest in sight, not even a clump of trees. I sighed and chewed at my upper lip. For the first time, my Nicorette patch failed me. I was desperate for a cigarette. I'd gone three days now, because Katie hated smoking.

The patch itched on my shoulder and I craved the inspiration of nicotine. Maybe it wouldn't hurt, just to have one. I walked back to the centre where I knew I could find a newsagent beside the Hippodrome theatre. I passed a building of glass and a movement caught my eye. I stepped up to the window and saw a huge white butterfly flapping in frustration at its invisible prison. I thought I knew how it felt. It was curious to see such a huge insect; the building must be heated. I stepped back for a better view and my heart leapt. I was staring at Wildwalk, a living rainforest in the heart of the city. Even before I reached the centre I knew the answer to her third clue.

"You need to find the king of the sea," she'd said. Yesterday it had drizzled with rain. We'd huddled together beneath her umbrella. I loved the warmth of her arm beside mine. Touching her made her more real, gave another memory to chase away the fears which haunted the long, empty hours without her.

"Easy," I said. "And tomorrow I'll know everything I need to find your home."

"Hah, don't be so cocky." She turned to face me and I struggled to hold back a kiss. "My final clue is as hard as nails."

I stood before Neptune and wished he could speak. His lips were frozen behind his beard and his cold brass eyes stared out to sea. Now I was lost. There were no more clues, only memories of the exquisite torment of loving Katie.

I felt foolish and very lonely amongst the crowds of smiling people. Bristol was vibrant, alive with young people. I wanted to share that life, to join with them in their love and laughter. I had chosen speed-dating because I was still too self-conscious of my foreignness. I wasn't comfortable with this country's mannerisms and hidden language. I thought five minutes an ideal way to get a snapshot of a person. There had been other girls I liked, ones who a measuring heart would find more suitable. One girl, a well spoken blonde, had been scented with the perfume of money. She should have been the one I phoned. I worked as a bus driver for First National, just one of many Eastern Europeans invited to fill a current labour shortage. I could never afford to buy a home on a single wage. That had been my first shock on arriving in Bristol, with its property prices rivalling London.

Katie had just left Bristol University. I hadn't asked her, but guessed there was a fair chance she'd be among the thousands saddled with huge debts to pay for their education. Her thesis had been on censorship. It was the first inkling I had of the sharp mind within. Her voice, though, was soft, seductive, always teasing. Katie had chosen me. She stole into my heart, my thoughts, and robbed me of choice. I'd felt bewitched and called her as a kind of compulsion.

"Come on, ladies and gents, this is my last one. Buy this and I can go home." A street vendor interrupted my sad reverie. "*Big Issue*, anyone?"

I was suddenly homesick. I'd postponed my holiday to spend time with Katie. I longed to see the open-air cafes and artists of my home city. I'd lost a week already, a week I could have spent with my family. I thought of Katie's last words and shook my head.

"Nails," I said aloud, without realising.

"You after the Nails, sir?" I turned to see the narrow-faced vendor staring at me.

"What?"

"The Bristol Nails – they're just up there, sir," he said, pointing to a busy junction. "Just bear left, you can't miss them."

Still I hesitated.

"It's not a wind-up," he said. "The Nails is where the old merchants used to hammer out their deals."

I stared at him, my mouth gaping. Katie had given me today's clue yesterday. She wanted me to call on her today. I was filled with a twisting whirlwind of emotions; admiration for her cunning, pure elation, but above it all a huge gratitude for this stranger. I bought his last copy and hurried along to the Nails.

"God bless you, sir," he called after me.

It started to rain again and I used the *Big Issue* to shelter from the heavy drops. They rattled loudly on the paper and seemed to wake me. Even before I reached the Nails I knew something was wrong.

The Nails, four huge brass tables which looked like they'd been turned on a lathe, were in a market place. The same market place I had started out from. I was a few yards from our little courtyard. I walked around to its entrance on the street just to make sure.

On the pavement was an information kiosk, a computer terminal mounted in a grey box splashed with red. It had a scrolling screen. 'Lost?', 'All The Stuff You Need To Know' and 'Need Directions?' flashed by to taunt me. I stepped up to the kiosk and ran through the options. There were helplines for Women's Aid, Childline, Crimestoppers and even Tide and Time information. There was a national missing persons option but somehow I didn't think that would help me. There was lots more information on entertainment, travel and leisure, but the thing that excited me was the maps. I quickly found the area I had just wandered around. The road with the cranes was called Hotwells Road. The name triggered another of Katie's clues, something I had dismissed because I didn't understand it at the time.

"When you're on my road you'll know you're getting warm."

Katie had reversed the order of the clues. Her home lay on the other side of the cranes.

I was breathless when I found them again. I continued down the road, past the choking fumes of gridlocked cars. I walked past modern apartment blocks on my left, shabby council tenements on my right. A little farther on I found the SS Great Britain.

And directly opposite was a beautiful little row of buildings, shops with attic rooms and balconies above them. The one in the centre was called Ginger. I knew enough curious English colloquialisms to know that redheads were sometimes called ginger. I wondered why Katie hadn't used Brunel's famous ship as a clue. I suppose that would have been just too easy.

I knocked on her door, my throat dry, my heart hammering like I had Mike Tyson caged in my ribs. A stranger, a girl I had never seen before, opened the door.

"I, uh…" Words, beautiful, comprehensible words, fled from me.

"You after Katie?" she said.

"Yes," I said, the answer rushing from me in a hiss of relief.

"She's in the BRI; I've just come to collect a few things for her."

"The BRI?"

She looked at me as though I was from outer space, or retarded.

"Casualty," she said, making allowances for my heavy accent. "She's broken her ankle. I told the landlord them steps was dangerous. And she was in such a rush to meet someone this morning." She tutted and rolled her eyes.

Her name was Mel. She'd been Katie's flatmate for over a year and was also her confidante. Mel told me how upset Katie had been when the ambulance came to take her to the accident and emergency department of the Bristol Royal Infirmary.

"She was bawling her eyes out, like she'd lost something precious."

Mel took me to the hospital, a sad old building blackened with age but with a bright new wing in pale bricks sprouting from it. Above the entrance was a brightly coloured statue; metal circles on wires in green, orange, yellow, blue and purple. They might have been scissors or scalpels, or hoops for harassed doctors to jump through.

Katie sat in a plastic chair, her bandaged leg supported before her. She saw me and her face lit with a warmth that finally chased away my fears.

"But how did you find me?" she said, after I'd given her an awkward but luxurious hug. I paused, felt a little stung.

"I'm not that stupid," I said.

"I know that," she said and ruffled my hair. "But you didn't have the final clue."

"Yes I did, 'nails'."

"What?"

"The Bristol Nails," I said. "You told me yesterday."

"I haven't got the foggiest idea what you're talking about." Her enchanting face creased with puzzlement.

"You said 'hard as nails'."

"I meant the clue," she said, still frowning. "I was going to tell you about the torch outside San Carlo – something about you needing Olympic skills."

I began to laugh and before she could speak again we were interrupted.

"Miss Collins?" A nurse appeared beside us with a wheelchair. "The doctor will see you now."

I looked at my watch. We'd had six minutes together and I felt good. I'd cheated fate of an extra minute.

"Will you wait for me?" Katie asked, the nurse holding back.

"Does a frog have waterproof ears?" It was my turn to give her a little clue.

It looked like I'd be cancelling the second week of my holiday. Or perhaps Katie would like a little trip now that she was off sick from work, maybe a chance to compare a mermaid with Neptune.

Editor's Notes

Bristol Tales follows on from the success of the York Tales, published in 2004. Inspired by the Canterbury Tales, each of the short stories in that collection was introduced by a quote from Chaucer. Inspired by the York Tales, each of the short stories in this anthology is introduced either by a quote from a person with a clear relationship with the area or a reference to a piece of writing which sparked off the idea for the story. These quotes add an extra layer to each tale by reaffirming the bond the anthology has with Bristol. Again, as with the York Tales, the authors were also given explicit parameters in which to work. Each story was not only to reflect the physicality of Bristol and capture the essence of the people who live and work there, but also the subject or theme of each tale was to reveal an aspect of life here and now.

When choosing the stories for inclusion in the collection, I was therefore looking for tales which would not only captivate and enthral, but which would, when viewed as a whole, be connected and contrasted – in the same sense that contrasting individuals connect to create a society. Each narrative had to be unique, its idiosyncrasies sketching a scene that would be both revealing and engaging. Bristol Tales forms a literary landscape where each view is different; whichever way you turn you'll find a distinct voice.

The variety of focus and tone, settings and themes to be found in this volume is testimony to the talent to be found in Bristol. The stories range from challenging and provocative to poignant and humorous. Some of the tales feature characters that are instantly familiar; some open a peephole into other people's markedly unfamiliar lives. The subjects alternate between the momentous and the incidental, yet each narrative provides a true snapshot of contemporary life. Every short story in this collection is a social observation; each is thought-provoking, insightful and instantly absorbing.

Although this collection of short stories is the result of a competition, it has been decided not to name the winning entries. It is not our intention to devalue the competition or the stories to which prizes were awarded, but rather to recognise the merit and diverse qualities of *all* the tales chosen for inclusion. I hope you enjoy reading them as much as I've enjoyed working with the authors who wrote them.

Rachel Hazelwood

Acknowledgements

W e are delighted to acknowledge below the many people and organisations who released permission to quote their work to the **TALES series'** writers and to us.

It was indeed a long labour to track down the many contributors who have been used to open the stories. In some cases, it was not possible to find the source of our preferred quotes and, in rare cases, we were unable to obtain permission. Our writers, who are undeniably creative, have, in a few instances, been flexible enough to either change their preferred quote or even, on occasion, quote themselves!

The copyright laws are complex and fraught with danger for a small house like END*papers*, and we have made every effort to comply with the legislation as advised. We are deeply appreciative to each of the contributors listed below.

The Tale of the Undivided Trinity by Daniel Doherty
The time of my departure is approaching.
Nigh is the hurricane that will scatter my leaves.
Tomorrow, perhaps, the wanderer will appear,
His eye will search for me round every spot,
And will not find me.
Thomas Chatterton, Bristol poet (1752-1770)

Hens' Tales by Lyssa Randolph
For all that it's dark
The city's routine claustrophobia lifts
As you tack across Queen Square
To where the harbour's laced
With isobars of neon,

Cash burning a hole in your pocket,
Desire like one in your guts.

The poem 'Nighttown' by Tom Phillips was originally published in 'City – Bristol today in poems and pictures' (Eds: Johnson/Hunter, Paralalia, Bristol, 2004). Copyright remains with the author.

Charlie's Tale by Alan Toyne

Women and cats, if you compulsion use,
The pleasure which they die for will refuse.

Thomas Chatterton, Bristol poet (1752-1770)
From a poem called 'The Romance of the Knight'.

A Tale of Angel Wings and Wine by Philip Jarvis

This story was inspired by a quote from a
local graffiti artist. Looking at the art and
realising it's graffiti, you question why you
should think it's important, then you realise
it's not a question of what's there,
it's what you've perceived that really matters.
Sometimes you remember to forget things when
all you need to do is hold on to those moments.

Philip Jarvis

A Blue Tale by Rachel Bentham

And if the crash comes?
I expect to meet you in the rubble,
half a brick in hand.
Here's mine.
Together we can build a crack.

From 'The Way We Are' by Philip Gross

The Interpreter's Tale by Maithreyi Nandakumar
How little do they see what is, who frame
their hasty judgments upon that which seems.
Robert Southey, Bristol writer (1774-1843)

The Daughter's Tale by Emma Edwards
This tale was inspired by a song by the band
Portishead who are a local Bristol band;
the song suggests seeing things
from a different perspective.
Emma Edwards

A Safari Tale by Alistair Spalding
Justice is always violent to the party offending,
for every man is innocent in his own eyes.
Daniel Defoe
Daniel Defoe was a regular at the Llandoger Trow
in King Street, one of Bristol's oldest pubs.

The Daydreamer's Tale by Louise Gethin
She remembers what's to become of her
as if it were yesterday.
'No. 4 Pickle Street', originally published 1988,
Fourth Estate. Copyright with Dave Peak

The Tale of Gregory Garland by Hayley Birch
…in my fancy…I climbed a thousand times
to that tall hill they call the Spy-glass,
and from the top enjoyed the most
wonderful and changing prospects.
R L Stevenson, 'Treasure Island'

A Rainy Day Tale by Laurajayne Friedlander

Today it has rained like people
Thin and newly alive
Then thick, heavy and old
The water came down like places
A drizzle of beaches
A deluge of mountains
A flash flood of far away
It has been wet like feelings
A thunderstorm of hurt
A cloudburst of ache
Torrential memories.

Taken from the poem 'Rain'
by Laurajayne Friedlander, January 2002

A Tale of Discovery by Jane Taylor

An untitled poem about children playing outdoors
*by **James S Constant** captures the essence*
of this story.

The Tale of Juma the Rich by Polly Carr

The city is a place of continual motion
where things form and disperse
connecting and separating
the language you speak
may not be the one I understand best.

Fiona Hamilton
© Fiona Hamilton, from 'City',
published in 'City, Bristol Today in Poems and Pictures',
page 20, edited by David Johnson and Peter Hunter,
Paralalia, 2004

Laura's Tale by Darren Croucher
Let thy soften'd heart intensely feel.
Robert Southey. Bristol writer (1774-1843)
From 'Inscription 03 –
For A Cavern That Overlooks The River Avon'

The Caretaker's Tale by James MacVeigh
My Duties do not take up two Hours of the Day.
Thomas Chatterton, Bristol poet (1752-1770)

The Immigrant's Tale by Steve Probert
She has made me half in love
with a cold climate.
Robert Southey, Bristol writer (1774-1843)

Author Biographies

(in alphabetical order)

Rachel Bentham

Rachel has been in Bristol longer than she's lived anywhere; the rainfall makes her stay in and write. She has stories and plays broadcast on BBC Radio 4, poetry internationally published and has recently finished her first novel. She lectures in creative writing at Bath Spa University, and walks her dog in the green spaces of Bristol and Bath. She is currently writing a play commissioned for Radio 4, for broadcast in spring 2006.

Hayley Birch

Hayley grew up in the Cotswolds. Her first book was sold at school for £1 a copy and provoked a cringing response on discovery after over a decade recently. Despite having lived close by for most of her life, she has developed a new-found fascination for Bristol and its people. Her tale was inspired by her love affair with the beautiful Old City and marries modern day Bristol with fantastical notions about the harbour's secret past.

Polly Carr

Polly was born in North Yorkshire, in a corridor. She used to live on a narrow boat. She has no sense of direction and can get lost in a phone box. Years ago, she arrived in Bristol (by accident) and loves it – although she has been wildly unfaithful with Dublin, Santa Fe, Prague and Tofino. Oh, and Bridgwater. Aside from the day job, she spends her time perpetrating poetry and short fiction.

Darren Croucher

Darren has an MA in Creative Writing from Bath Spa University College. While studying there, he completed a novel for young adults that he is adapting into a radio play. 'Laura's Tale' is the opening piece from a collection of linked short stories delving into the worlds of interconnected characters as the places they live in shape their lives. He is currently working on another collection of short stories linked together by a shared atmosphere.

Daniel Doherty

Daniel Doherty is an independent management consultant who lives – and loves to live – in Bristol with his wife Louise. His affair with Bristol began in 1969, when an undergraduate at the University. As the wheel turns full circle, he is now back at the University of Bristol studying for a PhD. The research approach involves auto-ethnography, which in simple terms involves the writing of his life, and attempting to make meaning of it.

Emma Edwards

Emma Edwards has lived in Bristol for most of her life. She resides in Redland and is currently studying for a Masters in Screenwriting at UWE, and dreams of writing fabulous books and films one day. When not studying she enjoys reading, cooking and walking. She is often found out and about in the clubs and bars of Bristol with her friends, protesting that she's getting too old for it, while refusing to be dragged off the dance floor.

Laurajayne Friedlander

Laurajayne moved to Bristol in 2001. A successful poet, her work was used to raise awareness for International Women's Day. Her poem 'Rain' was used to promote Bristol Poetry Festival in 2002 and in 2004 her poem 'In Bristol, in Love' was a prizewinning entry in the 'My Britain, My Bristol' competition. Laurajayne also tutors a creative writing group in the centre of Bristol. In 2005 her first screenplay 'Flowers' was short-listed for development funding by South West Screen.

Louise Gethin

Louise Gethin writes short stories and poetry. Recently, she won first prize at the Winchester Writers' Conference, for 'Innocent's Baby'. She has an MA in Creative Writing from Bath Spa University College, where she was involved in the editing team who published the student anthology *Watermark*. A keen photographer, she often uses pictures as inspiration for her writing. Her ambition is to publish a collection of short stories.

Philip Jarvis

Philip Jarvis was born in Portishead in 1982. At Bristol University, he studied English and Information Systems for two out of three years, the remainder of the time spent in the USA working with touring theatre companies. He still managed to graduate somehow. After a spell working in theatres in Bristol, he now works in a bookstore. As well as writing, he likes to make music or noise using a ukulele, bass, a violin, keyboards or whatever is on his desk at the time.

James MacVeigh

James MacVeigh started writing in 1982 with a biography called *Gaskin*, published by Jonathan Cape, which was made into a BBC film starring Paul McGann. He has published over thirty short stories in magazines and anthologies and had one broadcast on Radio 4, which also produced one of his plays. His stage play, *Chatterton*, was produced at the Bristol Old Vic in 2000. He's written an erotic novel but will not write another. His recently co-written biography, *A Boy Called Graham*, is set partly in Bristol. Its subject died of Aids while serving life for murder in Full Sutton prison, York.

Maithreyi Nandakumar

Maithreyi Nandakumar moved to Bristol twelve years ago from Madras in India. She's worked as a presenter for BBC Radio Bristol, a journalist for BBC Points West and is a freelance reporter for Radio 4 programmes. She began to take her writing seriously after starting Vivida, a writing group for Asian women in the Southwest two years ago. 'The Interpreter's Tale' is an extract from her novel (a work in progress), *Stirring the Pot*, that explores the lives of three friends from Madras who now live in three different continents.

Steve Probert

Steve is forty-two years old and lives in Bristol. He has a Diploma in Creative Writing from Bristol University. The diploma encouraged him to try different kinds of writing and he's had a short story published in the *Evening Post*. He likes to read a wide variety of mostly contemporary authors. He works as a postman, which keeps him fit and gives him lots of time to think about his writing. He's in the process of editing his first novel.

Lyssa Randolph

Lyssa Randolph is a writer, researcher and teacher. She has a PhD in English Literature and her thesis examines the use of scientific discourses in the writing of a variety of women writers of the late nineteenth century; her co-authored book, *New Woman Writers*, will be published by the British Council and Northcote Books in 2006. She has taught Victorian fiction at University College Worcester and Bath Spa University College, and is currently a visiting lecturer at the University of Wales, Newport, where she teaches on the MA in English Literature.

Alistair Spalding

Alistair studied English Literature and Cultural Criticism at Cardiff University, also doing modules in Creative Writing. After finishing university he moved to Norway, living in Bergen for a year where, amongst other things, he taught break dancing to school kids. Next he spent a year in Melbourne, Australia, where he first started working in bookstores. Now, still unsettled, he is working in another bookstore in Bristol. He is currently discussing a children's novel with publishers.

Jane Taylor

Jane has been a teacher of English as a second language for seven years, teaching in Canada, Argentina and Nottingham before settling in Bristol. For the last year, she has been a full-time lecturer at City of Bristol College, teaching and organising the English language classes for refugees, asylum seekers and immigrants. She has recently started entering competitions, and a short story she wrote for the *Chalkface Goes Further* series on BBC Radio 4 was broadcast last Christmas.

Alan Toyne

Alan travelled extensively during his early twenties and arrived in Australia in 1994. He lived in Melbourne for several years, where he wrote various travel-related articles and a short novella about backpacking in Thailand. In 1997 he became the joint winner of the *Guardian* and BBC Radio 5's Young Travel Journalist of the Year award. The prize was to produce a travel article about Croatia and a short radio programme. He is working on his first novel, a series of six linked first-person-perspective novellas, set in Hackney, Ecuador and Peru.

About the TALES series

If you are interested in how a **TALES** anthology might be launched in your area then by all means contact us at *info@endpapers.co.uk*, and of course be sure to check out the other titles in the **TALES series** and look out for forthcoming volumes on *www.endpapers.co.uk*

We launch short story competitions as a catalyst for local writers. We use the competition as a means to attract writers' attention to the very real possibility that their work might be published to wide acclaim within one year.

The **TALES series** represents a commitment to new writers and to 'villagisation' as opposed to 'globalisation'. We are all probably grateful for the smaller world we can now travel through more easily and more cheaply. Many of us doubtless enjoy the benefits of wider and wider availability of everything. What the **TALES series** has shown us, however, is that there is nothing quite like the local story, with a familiar backdrop, to engage our interest.

In 2004 we published **YORK TALES** which acted as our prototype.

In 2005 we have **BRISTOL TALES, GLASGOW TALES** and **TYNESIDE TALES**.

In 2006 **SHEFFIELD TALES** is already committed and we are in the process of selecting other areas in Northern Europe for this third batch.

There is no end to the creativity of storytelling and the joys it can bring writer and reader, and indeed publisher. We look forward to working with new writers across the world for years to come.

Magdalena Chávez
Creator of the **TALES series**

Book Club Notes

Book Club Notes